e

"I was hoping—" ~~eyes~~ as he contin~~ued~~ have dinner with~~

She was so disarmed~~ wrapped up in an incredible surprise visit at ~~her~~ rodeo and the little jump of her heart when she had first seen him.

"All right," Dallas said with a nod of her head.

"All right?" He repeated her response as a question as if he didn't believe her the first time.

This small sliver of insecurity in a man who always seemed perfectly secure made her smile at him. "I'd like to. Yes."

The idea of sharing a meal with Nick instead of spending the night alone, mentally rewinding and reviewing her mistakes in her head, sounded like the best alternative option she'd had in a long, long while.

"We could eat here, if you have the kind of stomach that can handle the-greasier-the-better rodeo food."

"I have a room at the Omni downtown." Nick pushed away from the trailer and took a step toward her. "Their steak house is supposed to be one of the best in Fort Worth. How does that sound?"

A thick, juicy steak or the stale ham sandwich she had leftover from lunch?

"Like a good idea."

THE BRANDS OF MONTANA:
Wrangling their own happily-ever-afters

Dear Reader!

Thank you for choosing *Thankful for You*! This is my eighth Special Edition book featuring the Brand family, and I couldn't be more proud.

Thanksgiving was my mother's favorite holiday because it was a time when the family came together to cook and eat and be thankful for each other. My mom was a wonderful cook, and as I am sure it is with your own family's Thanksgiving dishes, I was partial to my mother's famous sage-bread stuffing, hand-peeled smashed potatoes with lots of butter, her homemade apple pie and her one-cup salad! Yum!

One-cup salad is so easy to make that even a disaster in the kitchen like me can make it! Here's all you need:

Ingredients:

1 cup mini marshmallows
1 cup shaved coconut
1 cup canned mandarin oranges (drained)
1 cup canned pineapple chunks (drained)
1 cup sour cream

Directions:

Put all ingredients into a large bowl.
Fold ingredients together.
Chill in the fridge.
Serve and eat!

I invite you to visit my website, joannasimsromance. com, and while you're there, be sure to sign up for *Rendezvous Magazine* for Brand family extras, news and swag. Part of the joy of writing is hearing from readers. If you write me, I will write you back! That's a promise.

Happy Thanksgiving!

Joanna

Thankful for You

Joanna Sims

◆ HARLEQUIN® SPECIAL EDITION®

Recycling programs
for this product may
not exist in your area.

ISBN-13: 978-0-373-65995-1

Thankful for You

Printed in U.S.A.

Joanna Sims is proud to pen contemporary romance for Harlequin Special Edition. Joanna's series, The Brands of Montana, features hardworking characters with hometown values. You are cordially invited to join the Brands of Montana as they wrangle their own happily-ever-afters. And, as always, Joanna welcomes you to visit her at her website: joannasimsromance.com.

Dedicated to my sister from another mister...
Jacqueline
You are the best kind of friend and I love you.

Chapter One

"I'm looking for a Dallas Dalton." Nick Brand stood in the doorway of one of the bunkhouses on Bent Tree Ranch reserved for wranglers.

"Hey, Dally!" one of the wranglers, who was only wearing cowboy boots and a towel wrapped around his waist, bellowed over the loud talking of his bunkmates. "Door!"

Nick took off his mirrored sunglasses and tucked them into the front pocket of his navy suit jacket. He looked out of place, walking around his aunt and uncle's Montana ranch wearing his regular business clothes. He knew that. But he wasn't in Montana on vacation from his Chicago law firm; he was here on business.

Another wrangler, a short, stocky young man dressed for ranch work, announced his arrival again.

"Dally!" The wrangler grabbed a hold of the edge of a top bunk and shook it hard.

"Christ on a crutch! *What*!" Dallas popped upright like a jack-in-the-box.

The wrangler pointed at Nick. "Stiff. Eleven o'clock."

Dallas fought to get her wild brown hair out of her eyes; after letting out a grunt of frustration, she kicked off the covers, swung her legs over the edge of the bunk and then jumped down. Barefoot, but still wearing ripped jeans and a faded Johnny Cash T-shirt, she walked over to wear Nick was standing.

Confused, Nick said, "I'm looking for a Dallas Dalton."

Dallas wiped the sleep out of her eyes and then yawned loudly before answering. "You found her."

Nick stared at the woman's black fingernail polish, confused. "You're Dallas Dalton?"

Dallas squinted at the sun coming in the bunkhouse through the doorway. "Twenty-four-seven."

Nick shook his head; he pulled his sunglasses out of his pocket and put them back on. "I think there's been a mistake. I apologize for the interruption."

Dallas yawned again with a nod. Nick turned to leave, but Dallas stopped him. "Hey—hold on—are you Nick?"

Nick turned back toward the disheveled woman. "I am."

Dallas stretched her arms over her head, which drew Nick's attention, for a brief moment, to the woman's perky, braless bustline.

"You're in the right place." Dallas extended her hand. "Hank told me to expect you yesterday."

Behind his mirrored sunglasses, Nick stared at Dallas's face. Her handshake was as strong and as firm as any man's handshake.

"I was delayed," Nick offered. "I was expecting a man."

"Yeah. You're not the first," Dallas said.

She pulled a ponytail holder out of the front pocket of her jeans, clenched it between her teeth, gathered up her unruly mass of mahogany curls and secured them into a thick ponytail. Several tendrils escaped the ponytail holder and snapped back into position around her oval face. Nick had to consciously resist the temptation to tuck those wayward tendrils behind Dallas's ear.

"Let me grab my stuff and we'll head out," she said.

Nick waited for Dallas just outside the door of the bunkhouse. Dallas reappeared wearing a cream-colored straw cowboy hat and carrying a pair of brown boots that were caked with dried mud.

"You been in town long?" Dallas yanked on one boot and then the next.

"First day."

Dallas stomped her sockless feet farther into the boots, knocking some of the mud off. Satisfied, she looked up at him. "Ready?"

Nick followed Dallas to an early-model brown and tan Ford Bronco.

"It's unlocked." Dallas nodded to the passenger door.

Nick had to pull hard on the stiff door to open it, and the hinges squeaked loudly when he pushed it open far enough for him to get into the passenger side.

"I haven't seen one of these in years." Nick slammed the door shut.

"Bessy and I've been together since I was fifteen." Dallas grabbed a stack of papers on the bench seat and tossed them into the backseat. "She's a classic."

Dallas's idea of a classic and his idea of a classic were completely different. While Dallas shifted into Reverse, Nick examined the inside of the Bronco. The interior had been stripped—there wasn't a radio or air-conditioning system, part of the dashboard had been removed, exposing a tangle of wires that no longer served a purpose. Dallas obviously used the Bronco for more than driving, which was evidenced by the clothing, blanket and pillows strewn across the backseat.

Dallas used the crank handle to roll down her window. Nick followed suit and rolled down his window, as well. He rested his arm on the edge of the open window, glad for the fresh air.

"Did Hank fill you in?" he asked.

Dallas nodded and stepped on the gas. The cowgirl was not a cautious driver—she sped along the driveway, kicking up loose gravel and dust, the oversize wheels disconnecting with the ground as they took a series of bumps. Nick looked around for a seat belt but didn't find one; instead, he gripped the window frame with his hand and hoped that she had more control of the old Bronco than it seemed. At the end of the driveway, Dallas slowed down but didn't bother to come to a full stop before she pulled out onto the main road.

"Do you work for my uncle full-time?" Nick asked, glad that they were on paved road.

"Not me. I'm just workin' here until I save up enough money to get back on the barrel racing circuit." She patted the cracked dashboard. "I hope old Bessy here can make it for one more tour."

A barrel racer. That made sense. She was independent, confident and tough enough to live with a bunkhouse full of cowboys.

"Professional?" he asked.

"Since I was seventeen."

"Can you make a decent living doing that?"

"Some do. I don't. Most of my winnings go right

back into travel expenses and taking care of my horse. I'm lucky if I break even, but most years I'm in the hole." Dallas laughed. "How 'bout you?"

"I passed the Illinois state bar exam last month. Once I'm done with my business here, I'll start working at my father's law firm."

"Nepotism." Dallas nodded. "I can dig it."

The cowgirl continued, "I haven't been back to Lightning Rock since my pop died. Not sure how it's gonna feel goin' back there now."

"Davy Dalton was your father?"

When Dallas nodded, Nick continued, "I'm sorry I didn't make the connection earlier."

"Don't worry about it. Not much of a family resemblance there."

Nick looked over at his chauffer. The sun had bronzed her skin; her shoulders and arms were muscular, as were her thighs. She wasn't overweight, but she was stocky. Her fingernails were clipped short and the only jewelry she wore was a small turquoise cross on a silver boxed chain around her neck. She didn't necessarily look it, but Dallas came from rodeo royalty. Davy Dalton, a legendary bull rider, had been a longtime friend to his uncle Hank.

Nick was about to offer his condolences when Dallas made a sudden right-hand turn onto a heavily pitted dirt road. They immediately drove through a deep dip in the road and this time, Nick left his seat and had to put his hand on the roof of the Bronco in order to stop his head from smacking up against it.

"It's a bit bumpy," Dallas acknowledged, but didn't slow down.

Nick wanted to ask her to ease up on the gas pedal,

yet he couldn't bring himself to do it. It seemed out of step for the man to ask the woman to take a rocky road more gently. If this cowgirl could take it, so could he. He simply hoped that the road to Lightning Rock was short. He had spent a couple of summers at Bent Tree when he was a kid; Bent Tree held thousands of acres, so there were many areas of the ranch he'd never seen. Lightning Rock, fifty acres of high ground, was new to him.

A couple of S curves later, Dallas stopped in front of a rickety fence with a gate that was half off its hinges.

"We'll walk it from here." Dallas turned off the engine. "We've been slammed by rain lately—Bessy's too heavy. She's bound to get stuck in the muck."

Nick nodded his understanding. He hadn't exactly planned to be walking around in the mud, but he could adapt. He took off his jacket and rolled up the long sleeves of his light blue shirt. Together, they walked through the narrow opening between the sagging gate and the rotted fence post. As far as the eye could see, grassy knolls abutted hills with craggy gray and white rock pinnacles, and farther still, majestic snowcapped mountain ranges. It felt as if he had stepped into paradise on earth.

"Look." Dallas pointed to a flat expanse of land, knee-high with golden, willowy brush. A small group of moose was moving slowly through the grassland.

Nick spoke his thoughts. "I feel like I've just discovered heaven on earth."

"You have." Dallas continued on her way. "I can't believe you're gonna sell it."

Nick didn't answer immediately. After a minute, he

said, "My father has a responsibility to do what's best for my aunt's trust."

Dallas disagreed. "Selling off the crown jewel of Bent Tree can't be what's best."

Nick heard her but didn't continue with that topic. The fifty acres of pristine Montana land that was Lightning Rock had been heavily disputed by the Brand family since the untimely passing of his paternal grandfather. His uncle Hank had inherited the bulk of Bent Tree Ranch; any parcels of land he hadn't inherited, he had purchased outright from his three siblings. Hope, his only aunt on his father's side, who had died young from breast cancer, had inherited Lightning Rock. Upon her death, his father had become executor of her estate and trust, including managing control of the fate of Lightning Rock.

"There she is…" Dallas pointed to a tall cluster of rocks jutting out from the apex of a mound a short distance away. "Lightning Rock."

"Do you want to head that way?" she asked.

Nick nodded. He had been curious about the namesake of this parcel of land. It was an anomaly—a cluster of rocks that had been struck by lightning so many times that the quartz veins that crisscrossed the surface of the rocks had been turned into petrified glass. As they approached the rock formation, Nick realized that the family of rocks was much larger than he had originally thought. Lightning Rock was as wide as a midsize car and at least twelve feet in height.

"There's a perfect spot to sit down at the top." Dallas put her foot into a foothold and started to climb Lightning Rock.

Nick, although he hadn't really climbed anything

since he was a teenager, followed her lead. At the top of Lightning Rock, there was an indentation that was an ideal place to sit and watch nature's drama unfolding all around the landmark.

"Look at all of this fulgurite." Dallas traced her fingers along the veins in the rock. "It's everywhere."

Every time lightning had struck the cluster of rocks, the silica, or quartz, had turned to glass. From the sheer amount of fulgurite that could be seen with the naked eye, Nick imagined that the rocks must have been struck by lightning hundreds of times. This oasis, tucked away in the middle of Bent Tree Ranch, had inexplicably drawn the wrath of lightning for generations. For a little bit longer, they sat together on top of Lightning Rock, and then Dallas took him to the small homestead that her father, Davy, had leased from the Brand family. The homestead, tucked away in a forest at the base of a mountain, included a barn, a small cabin, a single-wide mobile home, an old yellow school bus and several antique trucks that were in various stages of decay. Dallas took the key to the mobile home off her key ring and handed it to him.

"You can go in if you want. I'll wait out here," she said.

Davy Dalton had died in the mobile home, so Nick could understand why Dallas didn't want to go in. He unlocked the door and entered the odd world of the rodeo legend. In that later part of his life, he had become a hermit of sorts. He didn't have visitors and he only went in to town when supplies were too low to be ignored. The trailer was piled high to the ceiling with papers and magazines and tin coffee cans and rodeo trophies. There was a small path leading to the back of the trailer, but Nick didn't explore past the foyer.

"Your father was quite the collector." Nick pulled the door of the trailer shut behind him.

Dallas half laughed, half snorted. "That's a nice way of puttin' it."

Nick slipped his sunglasses back on. "Is the cabin in the same shape?"

Dallas nodded. "And the barn and the bus and the shed. I don't know what drove him to do it, but no matter how many times I badgered him into cleanin' up the place, he'd just fill it up again. I finally just gave up and let him live his life how he wanted."

Nick spent a little longer walking the homestead, assessing the expense of cleaning up the property. He didn't know the whole story of Davy's final years, but it was sad to think of a rodeo legend ending his life on such a sad note. The last stop Nick made was the three antique Chevy trucks embedded into the earth.

"These are real heartbreakers," Nick said to Dallas when she joined him.

Dallas had her hands tucked into the back pockets of her jeans. "Pop always meant to get around to restoring one of these for me. He was going to fix up this middle one and use the other two for original parts."

"What year are they?"

"Nineteen fifty," Dallas said. "Nothing more than a heap a' junk now."

For Dallas, these trucks were almost her undoing. It was hard work not to let her sorrow show at being back at Lightning Rock now that her father was gone. Her stomach felt like it was jumbled up in a giant knot and tears of sorrow had been trying to push through ever since she first turned down that familiar dirt road. If she didn't get out of here quick, she'd end up bawling in front of Nick Brand, and that didn't suit her at all.

Dallas turned away from the trio of old trucks. "Ready to head back?"

She was relieved when Nick gave a slight nod of his head; she got the impression that he had seen enough to get a sense of the place: it was a mess.

On the way back to the Bronco, Nick said to her, "I was really expecting to deal with your brother. Won't he want any of his father's trophies?"

"You won't see Brian within a hundred miles of this place," Dallas said bluntly. "He hated Pop almost as much he hated life on the rodeo circuit. Blames Davy for all of his problems. Last I heard, he was working for Lowe's in the garden department."

Dallas smacked a bug that had landed on her arm, flicked it off, while she continued talking. "I always knew that I would be the one to tie up the loose ends of Davy's life. I'm his daughter, and I loved him like crazy, so…that's that…"

For the rest of the walk back to where they had parked, neither of them spoke. It wasn't until they were back inside the Bronco that Nick asked, "What's on your agenda for the rest of the afternoon?"

"Practice." Dallas made a quick U-turn and stepped down on the gas. "You can watch if you want."

He wasn't the only man who wanted to watch Dallas practice barrel racing. A small group of cowboys were hanging on the fence or leaning on the fence, which surrounded the practice arena. Nick positioned himself on the opposite side of the fence and waited for Dallas to start.

"You Angus's boy?"

Nick turned slightly to the left to see if the question had been posed to him. An older man with severely bowed legs, deep wrinkles carved into his face and a thick black mustache peppered with white stood next to him.

"I am."

The cowboy offered his hand. "Tom Ketchum."

"Nice to meet you."

"Your father and I go way back." Tom joined him at the fence. "You take after him."

Nick caught a glimpse of Dallas walking out of one of the many Bent Tree barns leading a sleekly built blue roan gelding over to the arena. She swung into the saddle and started to work the mare to warm her muscles. Once Dallas started to ride in the arena, all eyes were on her.

"She draws a crowd," Nick said to Tom.

"That she does." Tom chuckled. "I've trained her off and on since she was a kid, and it's always been that way."

The more Nick watched Dallas ride, the more he wanted to watch. She had that "it" factor—that intangible quality that makes the world stop and take notice without ever really knowing why.

"One of those cowboys a boyfriend?"

Tom rested his boot on the bottom slat of the fence. "Dallas isn't the kind to get pinned down. She's never let anything interfere with barrel racin'."

Dallas cantered by, and even though he knew that she saw him, her focus was entirely on her horse.

"She's ready, Ketch."

Tom pulled a stopwatch out of the pocket of his blue-and-white-checkered shirt.

"Watch this," Tom said to Nick.

Dallas cantered out of the arena, made a small circle and then halted at the arena entrance to wait for Tom's signal. Dallas's horse pranced in place, anxious to race toward the first of the three barrels placed in a triangle pattern. Once Tom gave her the signal, the rowdy cowboys quieted while Dallas galloped full throttle toward the first barrel. As Dallas rounded the first barrel, Nick heard her yell "Ho" to the mare. Once around the first barrel, Dallas urged her swift-footed gelding to gallop the short distance to the second barrel.

"Ho!" Dallas's voice was sharp and crisp and commanding.

"Now she'll head for the money barrel," Tom explained.

Once Dallas rounded the third barrel, all the cowboys started to cheer and wave their hats in the air. Tom stopped the stopwatch and looked at the time.

"I've seen her do better." He shook his head before he gestured for Dallas to go again. "Give her more leg when you go around the last barrel, Dallas! You're losing a ton of time letting her drift so much!"

Now Nick understood why Dallas drew a crowd— she was a dynamic, risky rider who was sexy as hell to watch.

"Can I give you a word of advice, son?" Tom asked without looking at him directly. "Never try to corner somethin' that's meaner than you."

Chapter Two

Nick hadn't been the only man to stay until Dallas was done with her barrel racing practice. In fact, most did stay. There was something magnetic about the cowgirl—she had that unexplainable "it" thing that made a man want to follow her with his eyes.

Later that night at his hotel room, Nick reflected on his odd fascination with the barrel racer. He had always been attracted to tall women—he hadn't gotten his father's height, so he tended to date women who were a little taller than he was. He liked his women leggy, with a healthy bust and a reasonable family pedigree so she would fit in easily at the country club. His parents had doted on him as the only boy, and he had been, for years, an unabashed playboy. After he barely squeaked out a diploma in business from Princeton, he'd spent the better half of his twenties yachting with his friends and spending time in Europe and Dubai.

He'd dated women from all over the world, but he couldn't recall a woman like Dallas registering on his radar screen. She was the total opposite of what typically attracted his attention: she was short, stocky, flat chested and had a mass of untamed brunette hair. She was—unkempt. It made him wonder if the fascination would stick. Would Dallas Dalton still be as interesting to him tomorrow as she had been today? Only time would tell.

"Howdy-ho!" Dallas called out to him the next morning.

"Good morning." Nick held up his hand in greeting.

The cowgirl walked toward him wearing a brown tank top, cutoff shorts that hit her midthigh and her cowboy boots.

"I decided just to bite the bullet and make camp here for a bit." She hitched her thumb over her shoulder toward a rickety paddock where her horse was trying to reach a piece of grass located on the other side of the fence. "Unless you mind, I'm gonna bunk here until we're done."

She stopped when she reached him, and that was when he felt it again—that magnetic pull toward Dallas. He usually looked up to the women on his arm, even taller in their high heels, and it was nice that he could look Dallas right in the eye, that she was shorter than he was by a couple of inches, at least.

"I was thinking the same thing." Nick surveyed the property with his eyes. The place seemed to be more of a mess than the day before. The trip back and forth from Helena to Bent Tree was going to get old quick.

"There's plenty of room," Dallas said. "But no luck with the trailer. It's a long ways away from livable. I think the cabin is our best bet if you want to bunk out here too."

They started walking toward the small cluster of

buildings near the trailer where Dallas's famous father had spent the last years of his life as an eccentric hermit. He didn't want to offend Dallas, especially after she had just recently lost her father, but the legend of her father didn't match the condition of his aunt's property. It didn't make sense that Davy Dalton could have ended up this way. Nick hadn't said the words aloud, and neither had Dallas for that matter, but the famous rodeo personality had been hoarding for years.

With fresh eyes, Nick stated what might have already been the obvious to his companion. "This may take more time than I originally thought."

Dallas nodded.

"I honestly don't know where to begin." He didn't normally feel overwhelmed, but he did now.

"Pop always said…the only way to eat an elephant is one bite at a time."

Dallas had worked side by side with men her whole life. Her earliest memories were traveling from town to town, chasing rodeo money with her dad. Her father had been one of the first of his generation of rodeo men to garner endorsements, so when Davy wasn't riding a bull or roping a calf, he was posing for pictures at tack and feed stores. She'd only really known the nomadic life because of Davy; he'd raised her his way on his terms. The schools were always after him about the huge blocks of time she was out from school, but her father believed that she could learn a heck of a lot more about life out on the road with him than she could locked up in a school for eight hours a day.

She had loved her freedom growing up and often felt sorry for her peers who didn't get to do as they pleased.

Davy was too busy making a buck or losing that same buck gambling to regulate her every move—she made her own rules, set her own agenda. Could her father have done better by her? Sure, he could have. What parent was perfect? And yes, her childhood had left scars—some too deep and jagged and discolored to ever heal. But she was as tough as any man—she wasn't afraid of much in life—and she was a survivor. She had Davy to thank for that.

"It's hotter than the dickens in here." Dallas lifted the bottom of her ribbed tank top up to her face and wiped the sweat off her face.

"Let's take a break," he suggested, and she agreed.

Although she had spent most of her life surrounded by men, none of them had been like Nick. In the short time she had spent with him, he had caught her attention in a way no man before ever really had. Nick was clean-cut, educated and a gentleman. And so handsome. Just like everyone else in his family, Nick had those shocking Brand-blue eyes, and she had found herself staring into them more than once. Yesterday during practice, she'd found it difficult to focus on her work with Nick watching her.

While most of her fellow barrel racers dreamed of marrying cowboys, Dallas had always wanted something different than what she'd known. She didn't spend a whole lot of time imagining herself married, but when she did think of a husband, it was to someone like Nick.

"You need gloves." Dallas fished a bottle of water out of her cooler and handed it to him.

Nick's once-well-groomed fingernails were black—his hands gray from the dust and the old print off the newspapers.

Nick looked down at his free hand as if he were noticing how dirty it was for the first time. He stared at his hand for a long minute.

"I admit," he said, "I didn't know what I was getting myself into here."

"No." She finished her water and capped the bottle. "I bet not."

Not only was Nick a handsome man, he was tougher than she had originally given him credit for. She had thought that the thick, stale, hot air, the dust and dirt, and the piles of decaying magazines and newspapers would send him packing pretty quick. But he had hung in there with her. She was impressed.

"I didn't even think about food." Nick squinted in the bright sunlight streaming in through the window.

"Your aunt packed a care package for me this morning. There's more than enough to share."

Barbara Brand, Nick's aunt, was the matriarch of the Brand family and self-appointed caretaker of the disavowed and disenfranchised youth. Nick's aunt had been looking after her, in one way or another, ever since she was a little girl.

They took turns scrubbing their hands in the cabin sink with a sliver of soap that had become cracked and chalky over the years. Then they turned a crate over in the yard for a makeshift table and salvaged a couple of creaky-legged wooden chairs out of the cabin; with the backdrop of the expansive, cloudless blue sky and mountain peaks in the distance, Nick joined her for lunch.

"Okay—let's see what we've got here." Dallas fished into her cooler for the care package.

"This looks to be smoked ham and Swiss on Barb's

homemade sourdough bread. And this one is…" She peeked inside the wrapping. "Roast beef and cheddar on sourdough."

"I'll take whichever one you don't want."

She wrinkled her brow at him with a shake of her head. She held out both sandwiches. "Pick."

Nick pointed to the roast beef.

"Perfect." She smiled at him. "I wanted the ham."

For the first several big bites of their sandwiches, neither of them spoke. They were too hungry to try to talk and eat.

"Hmm." Nick made a pleased sound after he had devoured the first half of the sandwich.

Dallas nodded her agreement, still chewing on a bigger-than-necessary bite. Barbara was known in the county for her cooking. If you were invited to Bent Tree to eat, you didn't turn the invitation down. She loved to cook, she was great at it and she always made enough for plenty of leftovers.

"I appreciate you sharing your lunch with me." Nick balled up the wrapper.

She nodded to say "you're welcome." "I think your aunt planned it this way. She's always thinkin' about everybody else."

"You seem to know Aunt Barb pretty well."

Dallas watched Nick stand up and stretch. He didn't have the height of the Montana Brand men, but he had nice shoulders and a fit body. Nick's sister, Taylor, was married to Dallas's best friend, Clint McAllister. Nick didn't much resemble his male cousins, but she could definitely see the family resemblance with his sister and she told him as much.

"I've heard that all my life." Nick looked down at

her with his lips turned up slightly into the smallest of smiles. "I got razzed pretty regularly about it by my friends. The worst days were when Taylor wore a dress."

"Why?"

Nick crossed his arms in a relaxed, resting manner. "Oh, you know… I'd hear things like, 'what happened to your pretty blue dress, Nicki?' Stupid stuff like that."

"Heck." Dallas stood up and tossed her wrapping onto the trash heap. "I get worse than that from those cowpunchers I bunk with part of the year."

"It does sound tamer than I remember," Nick said with a laugh. She liked how he could laugh at himself so easily.

Dallas stood next to the Chicago native wishing that they had met under different circumstances. She wasn't at her best right now—she was dirty and sweaty and smelly. She wanted Nick to see her as a woman, not as a work buddy.

"Are you ready for round two?" Dallas asked, half hoping he'd give up for the day.

"The sooner we start, the sooner we're going to finish."

They walked the short distance back to the cabin side by side.

"You must know Taylor from Bent Tree."

"No." She grabbed the pitchfork she had left leaning against the side of the cabin. "I know her 'cuz she's married to my best friend."

It must have taken Nick a minute to make the right connections in his mind, because they were back inside the cabin before he asked her, "Clint's your best friend?"

"Yep." Dallas stabbed a stack of papers with her pitchfork.

Out of the corner of her eye, she saw Nick lean on the handle of his shovel.

"You bunk with men and your best friend is a man? You lead an unusual life."

Perhaps he didn't mean it to sound condescending and judgmental, but that was how it sounded to her ears and that was how she took it. She didn't much care what most people thought about her life, but for some reason, it stung when it seemed like Nick was joining her naysayers.

She grunted as she lifted the heavy pile of newspapers and dumped them into the empty cart between them.

"It might seem unusual to some." Dallas turned away from him to stop him from seeing the hurt in her eyes. "But it's normal for me."

They spent the rest of the afternoon cleaning out the small cabin. Years of her father's life were spent "collecting" these papers, something he could never explain to her, and she was shoveling those years into a trash pile to be burned. She didn't feel sad too often—but *this* made her feel sad.

Dallas stood by the large pile of trash they had started, and she knew that this was just the beginning of what was going to be a painful journey of simultaneously discovering and discarding the secretive last years of her father's life.

Nick wheeled another cart over to the pile and dumped it with an exhausted grunt.

"I think I've had enough for today," he said to her. "How about you?"

More than enough.

"The cabin still's got a long way ta go." She expected Nick to suggest that they bring in a crew to clear off the land and just be done with it. She wouldn't blame him, but she prayed that he wouldn't. Her father still deserved his privacy. It made her heart hurt just thinking about strangers rummaging through his belongings, judging him.

"I'm not sure it's ever going to get there," he said.

She tucked her hands in her back pockets, glad that Nick was signaling that he was ready to leave.

"Well," he said after she didn't continue the conversation, "I'll see you in the morning, then."

"Yep."

He started heading to where he had left his rental car. But then she saw him hesitate.

"Are you sure you'll be okay out here by yourself?"

She didn't have the heart to tell him that she was way more fit to rough it than he was. He was a Brand man, albeit a citified Brand man, and it was his nature to be a gentleman.

"Go on back to Helena and get some rest," she tried to reassure him with a forced half smile. "We've got a full day ahead of us tomorrow."

He hesitated for a moment longer; he gave her a quick nod to let her know that he'd gotten the message she was sending.

Once Nick was out of earshot, Dallas lowered herself onto her haunches, her arms folded tightly in front of her body, her hands pressed into her stomach. All of this was so much harder than she had thought it would be. One minute she thought she was okay and the next minute she felt like crying. And, other times, like now, she just needed to be alone.

"Oh, Pop." Rare tears slipped onto her cheeks. "I miss you."

Nick stood under the showerhead, letting the hot water beat down on his shoulders until the water started to run cold. He hadn't ever worked that hard in his life. Not ever. And the only reason he had pushed himself as hard as he did was that Dallas was relentless and strong and he didn't want to appear to be a soft city dweller in front of her.

Damn, but she was determined and strong. He'd never seen anything like her before.

"Ow…crap."

His hamstring locked up when he stepped over the edge of the tub to get out of the shower. He half fell onto the bath mat, grabbed for his hamstring with one hand and the towel bar with the other.

After he got his hamstring to unlock, Nick hobbled, with stiff joints and an aching lower back, to the bed and flopped onto the mattress.

"Oh, man." He carefully stretched out his legs, wincing at the pain in his knees as they straightened.

He'd never been a jock or a muscle head, and he had been slacking off on his workout routine for the past several years while he was buried up to his eyeballs in law books—but he'd never considered himself to be a lightweight before. He felt like a total lightweight now.

Eyes closed, Nick rested his hands on his stomach and tried to rest. The day after you exerted your body was always the worst; tomorrow he imagined he was going to feel awful. Instead of falling asleep as he'd hoped, he started to think of ways to make the cleanup of Lightning Rock quicker. But the only two options he could come up with included bringing a crew of men in to help clean out the buildings *or* bringing in a crew to just demolition the buildings and be done with it.

Whenever he thought through either of those options, his mind would conjure Dallas's face. This was personal to her—these were her father's belongings. And even though most of it was just moldy, decaying papers, every once in a while, Dallas would come upon something in the rubbish that she wanted to keep. How could he take that away from her? How could he tarnish the legacy of Davy Dalton?

The answer to both of those questions, no matter what angle he came at the problem from, was *I can't.*

The next morning, Nick got a later start than he'd intended. He awakened stiffer than a starched shirt with an ache in his muscles, joints, neck and lower back that he'd never felt in his life. Even the palms of his hands hurt; they were red and rough from wielding that shovel all day. His hands had remained mostly callus free and he had been perfectly fine with that. Perhaps it had even been a badge of honor to be a part of the white-collar and blue-blood class. But after watching Dallas work like she could keep going until nightfall while he was sucking wind an hour into the cleanup, he'd decided some calluses on his hands were exactly what he needed. He could stand a little toughening up.

Nick packed his belongings, put them in the rental car and checked out of the hotel. If Dallas could rough it out at Lightning Rock, then so could he. He grabbed a fast-food breakfast on his way out of town, ordering an extra-black coffee for Dallas just in case.

When he drove long distances, he liked to take the time to think. Same when he was stuck in rush-hour traffic back home in Chicago. He didn't listen to music or books on CD. He always thought about his next move, his next big goal. His future. All the way out to Lightning Rock, Nick thought about the property, and what he might say to his uncle Hank when it came time to discuss the sale of Lightning Rock. Intertwined with business was Dallas. On his first night in Montana, he'd wondered if his interest in her, his *curiosity* about her, was a passing fancy. By his second night in Montana, he had his answer: no. It wasn't a passing fancy. She fascinated him. He was drawn to her. He wanted to know more about her—about what made her tick. He liked her.

And there was this one moment yesterday that he couldn't stop thinking over again and again: the moment when Dallas lifted up the bottom of her tank top to wipe the sweat off her face. It wasn't meant to be a tease—it was an innocent, practical move on her part. But that flash of pale skin on her toned stomach, so different than the reddish brown of the skin on her arms and neck, made his body stir and made his mind turn to sex.

"I was beginnin' to wonder if you'd decided to get the heck outta Dodge," Dallas said to him as she dumped the contents of her cart onto the trash pile.

"Don't think I didn't consider it." He was working hard not to walk in a way that would show how much hurt he was feeling. "I wasn't sure if you drink it, but I brought an extra coffee just in case."

"Been drinkin' it since I was ten." Dallas dropped the cart and walked over to him. "More of that unusual life of mine."

He caught her meaning and wanted to clear the air now that he had the chance.

"I think you have a great life, Dallas. Unusual isn't a bad thing in my book."

The cowgirl didn't respond to his comment, but he could read in her eyes that his words had hit their intended mark.

"It's black," he said of the coffee.

"I drink it any way I can get it," the cowgirl said to him as she took the cup of coffee from him. "Thank you for thinkin' about me."

She'd probably be worried if she had any idea of how much actual thinking he had done about her.

"I have somethin' for you too." The cowgirl pointed to his shovel resting against the porch banister of the cabin; a cowboy hat was hanging on the end of the shovel's handle.

"It was Davy's," she added.

Surprised by her thoughtful gift, Nick walked over to the cabin and unhooked the hat from the shovel's handle.

Nick hadn't spent time following bull riding since he was a kid—his interest stopped around the time his father and uncle Hank had their falling-out over the will—but, before that, he wanted to be like his uncle Hank, and his uncle Hank loved bull riding.

"Davy Dalton's hat." Nick held the aged brown Stetson in his hands reverently.

"And his gloves," Dallas added. "Flip it over."

Nick turned the hat over and saw a pair of work gloves tucked inside the inner band of the hat.

"If they don't fit, don't worry," the cowgirl said.

"I feel like these are things that you should keep," Nick replied.

"Why?" Dallas shook off his comment with a shake of her head. "They're too big for me, and Pop can't use 'em anymore. He'd think it was right that one of Hank's kin found some use for 'em."

Nick decided to take Dallas at her word; she didn't strike him as someone who spent much time talking around the truth. If she said it, she seemed to mean it.

He tried on the hat first and was pleased that it fit pretty well. Then he tried on the gloves. With a little stretching of the leather, they would suit him just fine.

"Thank you." He smiled at the cowgirl.

Dallas, who was pulling the cart back to the cabin, paused when she looked at him. A flicker of some emotion flashed quick and ephemeral, like a shooting star across a black sky. He couldn't read the emotion it passed so quick.

After a second, Dallas said, "Pop is pleased." And then she got back to work.

Chapter Three

It took them three days of sweaty, backbreaking work to clean out the cabin and get it rehabbed enough for him to bunk there with relative comfort. It had running water and electricity in from the main part of the ranch. It was humble, but it was habitable. Dallas had taken a break from training long enough to get him in the cabin; today, the fourth day of cleanup, she insisted on taking a break to practice barrel racing.

"How are you gettin' on?" Ketch asked him when he came back from giving Dallas some critiques on her technique.

Ketch was the only person Dallas had invited out to Lightning Rock. Nick had a feeling that Dallas didn't trust many people, including him, but she trusted Tom Ketchum.

"She's pretty quiet, most of the time."

Ketch kept his focus on his student. "She's been through a lot, that one."

"I think everything we've been doing out at Lightning Rock," Nick said about sifting through the remnants of Davy Dalton's life, "would be sad for anyone."

"Trouble is a private thing," Ketch agreed, then went back to coaching Dallas.

Nick watched Dallas with unabashed fascination. She was in complete control of her horse; sometimes she careened around the barrels so fast and so low that it actually made him hold his breath thinking that the horse was going to tip over onto her leg and pin her on the ground. She was fearless, her hair flying loose down her back, her cowgirl hat worn square on the top of her head. He hadn't thought she was beautiful when he first met her—cute, maybe. Now he had it in his head that she was one of the prettiest women he'd known. For sure, she was prettier on the inside than most he'd met. She was pretty on the inside like his sisters Taylor and Casey. That was the highest praise, as far as he was concerned.

"Woooo-weeee!" Dallas let out a loud whoop after her last barrel run. It felt great to be back in the saddle doing exactly what she loved to do. Blue's coat looked a shade darker from the sweat and he had white foam dripping from his mouth.

Dallas gave Blue some big pats on the neck to praise him for a job well done. She slipped her feet out of the stirrups, dropped the reins so her horse could have his head loose and she kicked her legs forward.

"He did better with a couple days off, Ketch!"

"He's lookin' good. He's gonna be ready to win big next time ye're in it."

Dallas picked up the reins to whoa her big blue roan gelding.

"He's tight and fast," Dallas said, her face flushed

bright red from heat and exertion. "I can't wait to get back out there. I can't *wait*!"

"When you plannin' on gettin' back out there?" Ketch asked.

Nick, from her point of view, was paying particular attention to her answer to that question. The only thing she wouldn't like about being back out on the road was the fact that she wouldn't be spending time with Nick. They had been building a friendship, a genuine friendship, out there at Lightning Rock, and she was going to miss him. She truly was.

Dallas swung out of the saddle and landed on the ground easily. She slipped the reins over her horse's head, loosened the girth and started walking over to the one spot where she could rinse the sweat off her horse's neck and back.

"I think I've just about got enough stuffed under the mattress to make a go of it once I'm finished takin' care of Pop's business."

Ketch stayed around to talk with them for a couple of minutes longer before he headed off to tend to the rest of his day. She finished rinsing off Blue before she turned him out with the rest of the horses. After such a great practice session, she really didn't want to ruin her good mood by tackling more of the cleanup.

Back at Lightning Rock, she said to Nick, "I'm so greasy and grimy, and the water pressure in that ol' outdoor shower Pop rigged up is as about as useless as tits on a bull. I swear I've got a week's worth of dirt in my hair that I can't get out. If I don't take a quick minute to jump in the lake, you'll be able to smell me from a mile away."

He smiled at her. "Let's avoid that."

She stood there for a moment, just enjoying the way it felt to have Nick Brand smiling at her. So handsome, that man. She got butterflies in her stomach whenever he watched her practice—she never got nervous around anyone when she raced the barrels, but something about Nick was different. Something about Nick made her *feel* different.

While Dallas grabbed a bottle of shampoo, a bar of soap and a threadbare towel, Nick pondered on the way Dallas had looked at him just seconds before. She had stared into his eyes and although the moment was fleeting, he had wanted it to keep right on going. She was such a complicated woman that it was hard to figure her out. Maybe that was part of the attraction. She was a challenge.

"You can come, if you want. I'm wearing a bathin' suit." Dallas said, "I don't suppose you brought anything to swim in?"

"No," Nick said. And now, more than ever before in his life, he coveted his few pairs of clean, dry underwear. Besides, wet white underwear in front of Dallas? The family jewels looked much smaller after an exposure to cold water.

"Do you want to swim?"

"Now that you've put the idea in my head, I'd love to get in the water."

"Go grab me one of your pairs of jeans, then."

He returned with his last pair of clean jeans; he'd been avoiding wearing them because they were brand-new and too expensive to use for the kind of dirty work he'd found himself doing of late.

"Give me a minute," Dallas said.

"Hey...what are you going to do with those?"

"Give me a minute," she said again.

Good as her word, she was back in about a minute. "Here. Go put these on and let's go."

Nick took his jeans from the cowgirl. His expensive jeans were now shorts. He didn't bother to ask her *what* she had done or *why* she had done it. That part was obvious.

"These were brand-new," he said.

"They're still new."

The way she shrugged made him believe that she was completely naive to the price of the jeans she had just ruined.

"They're just shorter. Go put 'em on."

Dallas peeled off her sweaty T-shirt, balled it up and dropped it on the bank of the small, clear-water lake. She sat down to yank off her boots as quick as she could. So hot, sticky and gritty. She couldn't wait to get into that cool lake water. Her luck and her curse were that she was focused to a fault. All she could think about after practice was cooling off in the lake.

"I'd thought that I'd been to all of the Bent Tree lakes when I was a kid," the lawyer said to her.

"It's always been my private spot." Dallas unzipped her jeans, shoved them down over her hips and legs so she could step out of them.

Dallas had strategically worn her old Speedo bathing suit under her clothing so she could get into the lake anytime she wanted. Her feet were tough from years of walking barefoot, so the pebbles and broken brush along the side of the lake didn't bother her.

"You much of a swimmer?" Dallas loved the feel of

the earth, warmed by the sun, beneath her bare feet. She always had, ever since she was a little girl.

Nick joined her by the edge of the lake. She glanced over at him as he peeled off his shirt. It was a quick glance, but long enough to notice how light the skin on his stomach was compared to the golden color of his arms and neck. He was a fit man; not ripped and shredded like a bodybuilder, but toned as if he spent some of his time, at least, working out. She seemed to like looking at Nick whether he had a shirt on or not.

"I was captain of my high school swim team."

His profile to her, Nick seemed to be taking stock of the clear-water lake.

"It's deep enough to dive from that boulder over there." She pointed a couple of feet away from where they were standing.

Not able to spend one more second in her grubby skin, Dallas tromped through the short brush, careful not to step on the Sweet William wildflowers that grew in brightly colored clumps along the bank of the lake.

The boulder was hot beneath her feet. To her, the burning was a challenge. The longer she could stand it, the tougher she was. And being tough, being able to handle her business alone in the world was a matter of survival. She didn't have anyone to depend on. Now that Davy was gone, she didn't feel like she had a family. The way her brother had treated Davy in his last years, like he was a pariah—that wound might scar over, but it would never truly be healed.

No. She was alone in this world.

Dallas stepped to the edge of the boulder, lifted her arms above her head and touched her fingers together like a steeple. With one strong vault, she arced into the air and cut the water with her hands with only the smallest of splashes. She knew this lake—had spent hundreds of hours in her youth swimming in this lake. This lake was her swimming pool; the banks of this lake were her playroom. At Lightning Rock, she was more at home than any other place on earth. She hadn't known how attached she was to the place—she hadn't realized how hard it was going to be to say goodbye to this beautiful slice of paradise—until she had begun to clear out her father's belongings. How many times a day had she stopped herself from tearing up? Countless.

Dallas touched a rock lodged at the bottom of the lake before she somersaulted forward to push herself up to the surface with her feet. She broke through the surface of the water just in time to hear Nick's warning.

"Incoming!"

Dallas was treading her legs so she could wipe the water off her face and out of her eyes. She opened her eyes just in time to see Nick performing a cannonball off the boulder. Nick landed a short distance away from her with a giant splash. Some of the water displaced by his cannonball hit her in the face. She sputtered a little bit, spitting out lake water and wiping the water out of her eyes for a second time.

"What score would you give me?" Nick asked after he swam over to her.

The man's arm strokes had been clean, strong and confident. She had spent so much of her time around rodeo men who had a propensity for stretching the truth a bit, she had half doubted Nick's claim to be captain of his high school swim team. But not anymore.

The cool, fresh water made her feel renewed. She

smiled with a laugh and held up two fingers playfully. "I had a better cannonball when I was nine."

"Oh, yeah?" Nick asked, treading water beside her. "You think you can do better? Show me."

The competitive spirit in her made her swim to the edge of the lake and back to the boulder to at least match, if not surpass, Nick's "city boy" cannonball. Without paying attention to the time, the two of them tried to one-up each other in the cannonball arena. They should have been heading back to the homestead and tackling the trailer, but instead, they frolicked together in the lake as if they had nothing better to do and all the time in the world. The early afternoon slipped away from them, and it wasn't until Nick called a tie that Dallas decided to let the competition end. She shared her bar of soap and shampoo with Nick, and they both left the lake a heck of a lot cleaner than they had gone in.

Together, they sat on the boulder to dry off in the sun. Sitting next to Nick, at one of her favorite spots in the world, felt as natural as being on the back of a horse. It didn't—couldn't—escape her notice that Nick had been making it easy for her to let down her guard. He liked her, she could see that in his eyes when he looked at her—she could hear it in his voice when he spoke to her—but he'd always been respectful. He'd always been kind. She couldn't remember the last time she felt so close to a man. Was she falling for Nick Brand? Her feelings were so mixed-up lately, she couldn't be sure. But, the nervous excitement she felt in her stomach whenever he stared into her eyes made her think that she might be falling for the Chicago lawyer. Hard.

"My sinuses are clear, that's for darn sure." Nick

pinched his nose with his fingers and shook his head a bit.

Dallas had grabbed her towel and had spread it out so they could both sit down without burning their butts and the backs of their legs.

"Mmm, I feel so good right now." Dallas tilted her head back to let the sun shine down on her face. "There's nothin' I like better than spending an afternoon swimming in Sweet William. This takes me back. It really does. Way back."

"Sweet William? That's the name of this lake?"

"Not the official name." Dallas kept her eyes closed. "But it's what me and Pop call it."

She opened her eyes and pointed to the flowers growing wild along the bank of the lake. "See all those flowers? Those are Sweet Williams. They love to drink up the sun and bloom in the summer. I love me some good ol' American wildflowers, don't you?"

An American wildflower. That's what Dallas was. Much like the wildflowers she loved so well, Nick had finally found a way to think about the cowgirl in a way that made sense to his brain. She was just as pretty and wild and hearty as those Sweet Williams growing on the side of a secret lake in Montana.

Sitting next to Dallas on that boulder, so close that he could smell the sweet scent of the soap on her browned skin, he couldn't think of a time in his life when he wanted to touch a woman as badly as he wanted to touch her. He wanted to kiss away the little droplets of water on her neck and her shoulders. He wanted to slip her modest bathing suit straps off her shoulders, just enough to kiss the water from between her modest breasts.

The cowgirl had been difficult to read, but the giant "hands off" sign she wore like a badge of honor was easy enough to decipher. If he tried to kiss her, which had been a thought in his head for a couple of days, she would freeze him out. They were friendly acquaintances now; if he made any sort of move that she interpreted as sexual, he'd lose that precious ground and then some.

Why did he care so much about preserving his budding friendship and trust building with Dallas? He wasn't entirely sure. Yes, he was attracted to her. But he didn't have any illusion of starting a lasting relationship with a wild-child barrel racer. His life plan and hers were at serious odds. He had tried to imagine Dallas in Chicago and had failed. So it had to be the challenge that Dallas offered to his ego. He hadn't always been the best-looking guy in the room, or the tallest, but he was decent looking, had blue eyes that women often gushed about, and he always had access to money and lots of it. Rejection wasn't something he'd had to deal with too often in his life. With Dallas, it seemed like a 100 percent certainty.

"I'd like to make a quick run back to the ranch for supplies. I didn't realize how bare our cupboards are," Dallas said as she came out of her horse trailer dressing room wearing a clean, ribbed tank top and pair of faded blue jeans. Her hair was still damp and blowing in curly wisps around her face.

His uncle Hank and aunt Barb had let Dallas "shop" at Bent Tree every week to stock up on supplies so they didn't have to make the trip to town. Would the supplies have flown so freely if he was the only one camped out at Lightning Rock? No. He was certain of that. His uncle

had refused to talk to him about the sale of Lightning
Rock; his uncle had refused to discuss easement rights
that would allow the new owner to travel across Bent
Tree land to reach Lightning Rock. So far, he'd been
happy to avoid that "come to Jesus" moment he needed
to have with his uncle. There was still so much cleanup
left to do. But he couldn't let his uncle put this off in-
definitely. Uncle Hank, who was known in his com-
munity as being levelheaded and fair, lost all of that
levelheadedness and reason when the topic of rightful
ownership of Lightning Rock came up.

"You comin' or stayin'?" Dallas put her cowgirl hat
on, which signaled to him that she was officially ready
to go.

Normally, he would steer clear of the farmhouse in
order to avoid any possible confrontation with his uncle.
Today, now halfway through the cleanup efforts, Nick
realized that time for avoidance was running out.

"I'll come with you."

If Dallas was surprised by his choice, she didn't show
it on her face. She was a woman who kept her cards
held tightly to her chest. Dallas had to know that she
was smack-dab in the middle of a family feud, yet she
never asked him one probing question. She kept herself
focused on tying up the loose ends of her father's life
and let him handle his own family business.

Dallas climbed behind the wheel of her early-model
Bronco and cranked the engine. Nick had been sub-
jected to the cowgirl's driving enough to grab the handle
above the window and hold on tight. She preferred to
be the one in the driver's seat—so did he. If they were
in Chicago *he* would be driving, but he was on her turf

now, and she had won that battle. On the rare occasion that they had to go somewhere together, she drove.

"You missin' your life back East?" Dallas asked him. This was about as personal as she had ever gotten with him.

"I do," he admitted to her.

He hadn't wanted to pressure her to go through her father's stockpile of possessions on a timer—this was part of her grieving process and he was trying his best to be respectful. He saw his friends having a good time on social media, he thought of all the work waiting for him at his new gig at his father's law firm and it made him miss life in Chicago. He missed fine dining and yachting and a comfortable bed. He missed his new Jaguar.

"Yeah." Dallas had one arm resting on the open window, her left leg bent so her boot was resting on the driver's seat. "I miss my life."

He'd already known that about her, so this admission was just confirmation. She had this restlessness about her. There was always a distance in her eyes, as if only half of her was really with him in Montana. There wasn't a boyfriend out there pulling her away— it was her life. It was the road. It was the competition.

"Do you have a place you call home?" Nick tightened his grip as they flew over a couple of bumps in the road. "Other than here, I mean."

Dallas gunned the gas, steering the loud Bronco onto the paved highway. "Not really."

Okay. Let me rephrase that question. "Do you have a place in mind to land once you stop barrel racing?"

Dallas laughed and glanced at him like he had asked

a very odd question. "I ain't never gonna quit barrel racing."

The next question he asked came out of nowhere for him, and afterward he was left wondering what had possessed him to even bring the subject up. "Do you want to get married? Have kids?"

"I haven't really spent too much time givin' it much thought."

The conversation stopped abruptly with that last question, and Nick discovered just how easy it was to step on a land mine with this woman. Most women weren't *offended* by the question of marriage and children even if they planned on building their career instead of building a family. Not so with Dallas Dalton. His asking her about her future status as wife and mother had seemed to touch a raw nerve.

"That's Clint's truck right there." Dallas nodded toward one of the trucks parked near the main house at Bent Tree.

Damn.

If Clint was at Bent Tree, there was a good chance his older sister, Taylor, was with him. He loved his sister—they'd always been close. But they were on opposing sides of the Lightning Rock issue and he didn't want to get into yet another battle of words with Taylor. He had stopped by his sister's house in Helena when he first arrived in Montana to meet his niece and catch up, but the minute the conversation had turned to Lightning Rock, they had gotten into an argument. He couldn't remember the last time he'd argued with Taylor.

"And that's Brock's truck right there." Dallas shifted into Park and shut off the engine. "It looks to me like you're in for a bit of a family reunion."

Nick nodded in response.

Both of his sisters, one older and one younger, had married Montana men and settled within one day's driving distance to Bent Tree Ranch. He had opted to not stay at Bent Tree to avoid conflict with Hank and he had begged off staying with Taylor or his younger sister, Casey, for the same reason. He'd been in Montana for the first time in years, and he'd spent most of his time there avoiding his own family. Maybe it was time to stop avoiding and start facing them. Maybe it was long past time.

Chapter Four

His sisters greeted him in the only way they ever had: with open arms. Yes, they disagreed about how to handle Lightning Rock, but that couldn't stop them from greeting each other with love. They had grown up in a home that was almost the exact opposite of the warm, welcoming feel of the farmhouse at Bent Tree Ranch.

Their house in the wealthy area of Hyde Park was a mansion; his mother insisted on keeping a full staff around the clock. Aunt Barbara, who had grown up in Chicago and run in the same social circles as his mother, prided herself on her cooking. His mother prided herself on having the ability to hire a personal chef. Hank and his father, Angus, were the closest brothers in age, but they couldn't be further apart in temperament. Angus was austere and withdrawn from the family; the more his marriage to Vivian fractured, the more time he spent at the office. Nick couldn't remember the last time he saw his parents show real affection toward each other. There was always tension crackling in the air when they were together—Nick often wished that they would just get a divorce already. So, very early on in their lives, it had been Taylor, Nick and Casey against the world.

"Nick." His sister Taylor used one arm to hug him while she held her daughter, Penelope, with her other arm. "I didn't know you would be here today."

"We're just in for supplies." Nick tweaked his little niece on the nose while his eyes shifted from one person to another until they landed on his uncle seated at the head of the long table in the center of the kitchen.

Taylor switched with their little sister, Casey, who stepped into his arms and hugged him as if she hadn't seen him in a long time even though they had seen each other when he first arrived in Montana.

"How are you feeling?" Nick asked his redheaded sister.

"I'm okay." Casey smiled up at him. There was something in that smile that he didn't believe. Casey had been diagnosed with uterine cancer and had undergone a partial hysterectomy. His younger sister had never made it a secret that she wanted to bear her own children; the cancer had taken that away from her and the family was watching her closely to see how she would handle it long-term.

One by one he made contact with everyone in the room. He had his hand clasped with the hand of his cousin Luke, a retired marine, when he saw Dallas come in to the kitchen. She walked directly to Clint, her best friend and Taylor's bull-riding husband; the cowgirl hugged Clint and her eyes were full of trust and happiness when she looked at the bull rider. Nick felt a twinge of jealousy at the closeness between Clint and Dallas—it made him wonder how Taylor, who was looking at

Dallas a little warily, could handle her husband having a woman as a best friend.

Aunt Barbara interrupted his train of thought. "This couldn't have worked out any better if I planned it myself. Why don't the two of you go get yourselves washed up? We were just about to sit down to eat."

It felt a little bit as if the universe had conspired against him, but he was happy to see his sisters and his aunt's kitchen smelled amazing. There was no sense passing up the delicious-smelling pot roast in the oven. He couldn't cook worth a damn and neither could Dallas.

"Go on." Aunt Barb tried to herd him toward the foyer so he'd hook a sharp left and wash his hands in the downstairs bathroom.

"Let me just say hello to Uncle Hank first."

A look of concern brushed over his aunt's face, but she let him do things his way. His way was to talk to his uncle without ruining his aunt's lovely dinner.

"Good to see you, Uncle Hank." Nick held out his hand to him.

Hank Brand, a man who closely resembled his own father, half stood up, shook his hand firm and brief and then sat back down.

"Go wash up like your aunt wants," his uncle said. "We'll have time to hash over things later."

Aunt Barb must've been working on her husband night and day—this was a huge change in his uncle's position. The fact that his uncle was even willing to sit down and discuss the future of Lightning Rock was better than he'd been willing to do for over a decade.

"Thank you, Uncle Hank." Nick gave him a nod. "I look forward to it."

That wasn't necessarily true. He wasn't looking forward to "hashing" things out with his uncle; he had resented his father for shirking his own responsibility and putting it on his shoulders. Yes, his father's caseload as a circuit court judge was jammed. But for once, Nick wished his father would "unjam" that caseload and put his family first.

Aunt Barbara orchestrated the seating and he took his seat between Clint and Luke.

"Dallas!" he heard his aunt holler above the din of the family talking among themselves, all voices mingling together in a loud cacophony. "Where are you going?"

Nick followed his aunt's sight line to where Dallas was just about to disappear into the foyer. "I've got work to do."

"You've got eating to do." His aunt shook her hand and gestured for Dallas to sit down.

Nick thoroughly enjoyed watching Dallas actually get outbossed by his aunt. Dallas ruled her own roost, but Bent Tree was ruled by Barbara Brand. Period. End of story.

Dallas hadn't planned on joining the Brand family for dinner, but she couldn't deny that she was glad Barbara had invited her to stay. Ever since she had been a little girl, eating at the Brands' had been a treat. This was the table where she learned what it was like to be a real family—with a mom and a dad who loved each other. And perhaps she would always felt a little bit like the girl with her nose pressed against the glass, even when the Brand family did everything they could to make her feel like she was an honorary family member. Either way, sitting down for a meal in the farmhouse was the closest thing to a typical American family she had ever experienced. Barbara's kitchen was buzzing with activity—loud talking, occasional arguing and so much laughter. Dallas sat quietly, watching, enjoying and soaking every second in.

The food started to get passed around the table, and Dallas's stomach started to churn with hunger and anticipation. Nick smiled at her happily as he filled his plate with heaping spoonfuls of mashed potatoes and smothered it with his aunt's gravy made from the pan drippings, pot roast with homegrown carrots and onions. For the first part of the meal, she noticed that Nick didn't talk—he just ate. Every now and again, Nick would make happy noises in between chewing and washing down the food with glass after glass of his aunt's homemade root beer.

"This beats our dinner prospects out at Lightning Rock, hands down," Nick said to her while he loaded some more food onto his plate.

It was Dallas's pleasure to watch Nick interact with his family. She could see how close he was to his sisters, how much they adored him, and it spoke well of the kind of man he was. A decent man. A good man. A man to admire.

A man to love?

By the end of the meal, Dallas had landed on one certainty – having dinner with Nick and the rest of the Brand clan would be one of her favorite memories.

After his second full plate of food, Nick felt satisfied enough to slow down and actually enjoy the third plateful of food and the atmosphere of his first family meal at Bent Tree Ranch since he was a teenager. It had always felt homey and welcoming here at the ranch; his aunt had a big hand in that.

He'd found himself comparing his mother with his aunt, and wondering how two women from the same place, the same neighborhood, could turn out so radically different. But they did. Aunt Barb always had something good cooking in the kitchen. She was a homemaker, wife and mother, and proud of it. This was what he remembered: good food and good conversation. Laughter. Family. He'd missed this feeling and all those childhood memories he had pushed aside when the family fractured after the reading of his grandfather's will bubbled to the surface. It had hurt to be separated from his aunt and his uncle. It had hurt not to be able to return to Bent Tree Ranch.

"Save room for dessert." His aunt, who had leaned over him from behind to take his empty plate, stopped first to give him a little hug.

Nick groaned. He knew he would have double helpings of whatever his aunt would be offering for dessert. No doubt it would be homemade, chock-full of sugar and butter, super delicious, and fattening. He didn't eat a lot of sweets even though he had a substantial sweet tooth. Law school required him to spend a lot of time sitting and studying—he didn't want to develop a "dad bod" this early in his life. But with all the physical exertion he was putting out just to keep up with Dallas out at Lightning Rock, he could stand to eat a slice or two of whatever awesome dessert his aunt had baked.

His aunt stopped next by her husband's side. She put her free hand on her husband's shoulder—Nick remembered how affectionate his aunt and uncle were with each other and it was nice to see that, like many things at Bent Tree, that hadn't changed either.

"Why don't you and Nick go have a chat while I get things ready for dessert?" he heard his aunt suggest quietly.

The expression on Uncle Hank's long face, a face that resembled Nick's father's in so many ways, shifted from satisfied to annoyed.

"I already had it in the works, woman. You don't have ta keep remindin' me like I'm Little Johnny who can't tie his own shoes without help. You manage your business and I'll handle mine."

Aunt Barb didn't appear the least bit bothered by her husband's sharp comment. She just smiled, gave Hank a quick peck on the cheek and then took his plate over to the sink.

Nick could feel his uncle's eyes on him; he had been trying to get Uncle Hank alone to discuss Lightning Rock, but Hank wasn't interested in opening up a dialogue. He was reminded of the phrase "be careful what you wish for" because the idea of sitting down with his uncle was making him anxious in a way that he didn't normally feel. But this was Uncle Hank—a man he'd idolized all his life—and he was talking about the one thing that his uncle loved only second to his family— Bent Tree Ranch.

His uncle balled up his napkin, dropped it on his plate, pushed back roughly from the table and stood up. Uncle Hank was a tall, slender man; the deep crevices around his eyes, on his forehead and around his mouth bespoke of a life lived in the sun. Even though he was eventually going to turn the operations of Bent Tree over to his middle son, Tyler, one day, Hank Brand appeared to be far from retirement.

Nick met his uncle Hank's eyes; his uncle, without a word, gestured with his hand for Nick to get up and follow him. Nick wiped his mouth with his napkin before he stood up.

"Hey," Taylor, always the mother of the siblings, said, "he's dad's brother – be respectful."

Instead of addressing Taylor's worry that he didn't have full control of the temper he'd had since he was a teenager even as a full-grown man, Nick merely said to those still sitting at the table, "Save my spot."

Nick followed his uncle into a small office off the kitchen. This was, as Nick remembered, Hank's sanctuary. It was the one spot in the house that Aunt Barbara didn't touch—no matter how disorganized or cluttered it became.

"Have a seat."

Nick closed the door to the office behind him and then sat down in a stout leather chair on the other side of his uncle's desk. The smell of the office—leather and unsmoked cigars—sparked memories in his mind that had long been forgotten. The last time he had sat in this office, in this same chair, he had been a kid. The chair that had seemed so mammoth years ago was actually just an average-sized chair; his uncle, who when he was a kid, seemed to be invincible and infallible, was just a man—a decent, hardworking, admirable man, but still just a man.

"It's really good to see you again, Uncle Hank." Nick thought he should break the ice with his true feelings. "I am sorry that what brought me back to Bent Tree is business that puts me at immediate odds with you."

Uncle Hank examined him with those bright, clear blue eyes that were a Brand family trait—a trait he himself had also inherited.

"I stopped smoking these." His uncle took a long cigar off a corner shelf. Uncle Hank ran the cigar under his nose and inhaled deeply; after smelling the cigar, his uncle put it back on the shelf.

"I had a heart attack a while back." His uncle rested his hands on his stomach and rocked a little in the high-backed chair. "Did you know that?"

Nick nodded.

The Brand family grapevine was alive and well on social media. Even though there had been a crater-sized rift between the three Brand brothers after the reading of his grandfather's will, when the cousins were old enough, social media connected them in protest of their parents' continued feud. So Nick knew that Hank had experienced a mild heart attack in recent years, which had encouraged his uncle to give up one of his favorite things: smoking cigars.

"Barb called your father when I was in the hospital," Hank said. "Angus never *once* picked up the phone to call me."

Nick had tried to talk to his father about getting in touch with his brother, but it was a well-known fact that Brand men were stubborn to a fault. Angus refused to call his brother until Hank apologized for accusing Angus of pressuring their ill father into changing his will.

"I'm sorry..." Nick started to apologize on behalf of his father.

Hank leaned forward, his crossed arms landing on the desk. "That's not for you to do, Nick. That's between your father and me. And that's where I wanted to keep it. I'm madder than a wet hen that Angus sent you out here." Hank stabbed the top of the desk with his pointer finger. "This was his mess to clean up, not yours."

"Dad has a full docket." Nick felt he had to defend his father. "I volunteered."

"We weren't raised to pass the buck, and Angus knows that as well as I do." His uncle stabbed the desk with his finger a couple more times to reinforce his point.

From the angry look on his uncle's face, Nick decided to let Hank gather his thoughts and wrangle his emotions.

"Now—I know you've been wantin' to sit down and get all this business with Lightning Rock squared away," Hank said after several silent minutes of thought. "I've needed time to mull things over a bit. I need to sleep on things."

"I'd like to know your thoughts on Lighting Rock," Nick said in a measured tone.

Anger flashed in Hank's eyes when he said, "There's only one ending, Nick. Lightning Rock belongs to Bent Tree. Lighting Rock stays with Bent Tree."

"I agree." Nick nodded, knowing that his next words were going to tick his uncle off like no other words could. "I've had a local Realtor pull comps on the land. Let's settle on a fair price for the land and we can put this issue to bed right now."

Uncle Hank clenched his jaw so hard that Nick could see the muscles bulging and moving beneath the weathered, tanned skin of his jawline.

The words that came out of his uncle's mouth were clipped and chock-full of decades of resentment. "I shouldn't have to pay one damn dime for somethin' that I already own."

This was an old argument—Hank insisted for years that the latest draft of his father's will clearly stated that Lightning Rock would remain a part of Bent Tree and that ownership of Bent Tree would be transferred to his middle child, Hank. That version of the will was disputed by the two brothers, Angus and Jock, and ultimately, that version was rejected in favor of the will that left Lightning Rock to the only daughter, Hope, now deceased.

"I know the history of this land," Nick responded in a neutral tone. "And I know how this piece of land has fractured our family…"

"That's not the only thing."

Nick nodded his agreement—there were a lot of old wounds between the Brand brothers that went back to childhood—but Lightning Rock was the stick of dynamite that blew the Brand brothers apart once and for all.

"Let's just settle this, Uncle Hank. Hope wanted the land to remain with Bent Tree—and the proceeds from the sale of Lightning Rock will be split between her daughter, her son and her four grandchildren."

Hank leaned forward again, his fingers threaded together and resting on the desk. He moved his clasped hands back and forth while he thought.

"I loved Hope," Hank said defensively. "This doesn't have anything to do with how much I love my sister. I didn't see Angus *or* Jock at their niece's wedding. *I* was there."

Nick thought it best to let his uncle get everything off his chest. They were in the office, which meant Hank was ready to end the feud and buy Lightning Rock from Hope's trust.

Hank yanked open a drawer to his desk, riffled through the hanging folders until he found what he was searching for. He sat upright in his chair and tossed a thick white envelope on the desk in Nick's direction.

"That's a survey of Lightning Rock and a check. That's my best and final offer, Nick."

Nick took the envelope but didn't open it. He stood up and offered his hand to his uncle. "Thank you, Uncle Hank."

His uncle gave his hand one quick, strong shake; as Nick left the office, he caught the eye of his aunt and gave her a little nod to let her know that all the work she had been doing to get her husband to agree to settle the issue of Lightning Rock had paid off.

"How'd we do?" his aunt asked when he approached her.

"We did really well, Aunt Barb." Nick put his arm around his aunt's shoulders and hugged her. "Thank you."

His aunt smiled a little while she wiped her wet hands off with a dish towel.

"Why don't you go on out to the porch and get some fresh air?" She reached for a dessert plate that she had saved for him. "And don't forget to take this with you."

Aunt Barbara had made his favorite—carrot cake. It was so good that he went back for another helping. He was scraping his fork across the bottom of his plate when Clint, his sister's husband and Dallas's best friend, came out of the house. Holding his new baby girl, Penelope, Clint sat down in one of the rocking chairs the Brands kept on the front porch.

"Man, your aunt can cook," his brother-in-law said with a full-bellied groan. "I can't never say no to seconds."

"I hear you, brother." Nick put his empty plate on the ground and noticed that his belt was cutting into his overstuffed stomach.

Clint, a rough-around-the-edges professional bull rider, had grown up in these Montana mountains. He didn't look like the fatherly type on the outside with his thick beard and tattooed arms, but by the way he was holding his baby girl, and smiling at her like she was the sun and the moon, Nick could see that his sister had married well.

"You wanna hold her?" Clint asked him when he caught him staring at a gurgling, babbling Penelope.

"Oh…thanks." Nick gave a shake of his head. "But no, thanks."

Clint's eyes crinkled at the corners and his lips smiled behind his beard. "I gotcha. That's exactly how I was until I saw Princess Penny here. She keeps my heart in her pocket."

Nick could see how attached the bull rider was to his baby daughter; unlike his sisters, he'd never really been all that sure that he wanted children. They seemed like a lot of work.

"I'm sorry I haven't been able to get my butt out to Lightning Rock," Clint said. "I don't know that you heard, but I snapped my collarbone down in Laredo. Rotten damn luck."

"Taylor did tell me." Nick nodded. "You've got to get yourself right."

"You're right about that—but I hate it that I can't be

out there to help Dally, man. Losing her pop's got to be tearin' her up."

Nick had seen firsthand in the kitchen how connected his brother-in-law was to Dallas; he had also seen that his sister wasn't entirely comfortable with the friendship. "You've known Dallas for a long time, haven't you?"

Clint kissed his daughter on both of her cheeks before he said, "Story goes, we shared a playpen, that's how long."

"You grew up together."

"Our pops were both rodeo bums—'cept Davy went and got famous and my pop just went and got drunk. Dally and me—we raised ourselves—we're as much family as anything."

Nick had wanted to ask Clint a question for a while, and this seemed like the best chance to get an answer. "Were you ever more than friends?"

"No. Never." Clint cradled his daughter in the crook of his arm. "She's like my sister. People don't believe us, but that's the truth of it. Unless folks growed up like we did, you can't understand where we're comin' from. She counts on me, I count on her and we don't let each other down. I feel like I'm lettin' her down not bein' able to get out to Lightning Rock. From what she tells me, you've stepped up big-time and I 'preciate it."

Nick was surprised, and pleased, that Dallas had spoken to Clint about him.

"It's hard for me to believe that she lets herself depend on anyone, she's so independent," Nick said half to himself, half to Clint.

"Dally's got a lot scars, brother. Some you can see

and some ya can't." Nick's brother-in-law caught his eye and looked at him as if he was sharing a secret. "Just 'cuz you can't see 'em don't mean they ain't there."

Chapter Five

In the end, Nick was glad that his family had come together. Even though his sisters and he disagreed on what constituted a good time, he would have made an effort to spend more time with them while he was in Montana if it weren't for the constant disagreement over the fate of Lightning Rock. Now that Uncle Hank was willing to settle the family dispute over this section of the ranch, the friction between his sisters and himself fell away as if it had never been there in the first place.

"Howdy!" Dallas galloped toward where he was standing.

The cowgirl didn't slow her mount as she approached him as if she were playing a game of chicken. It took all his guts to stand his ground and let her race, unchecked, in his direction. A couple of feet in front of him, Dallas reined her horse to a sliding halt. Lucky for him, the horse complied with the command and didn't run him over.

"I thought you were gonna flinch, for sure!" Dallas

laughed, her cheeks flushed red from the exertion of running the barrels.

The cowgirl looked so pretty to him when she laughed; it wasn't all that often, that was a fact, but she loved to run the barrels. She loved to train and compete. Those were the moments when he thought he caught sight of a woman inside Dallas—a woman whom she kept tucked away from the world. This was a woman he really wanted to get to know better—fun loving, sweet, happy. Unguarded.

Nick patted the sweat-soaked neck of the champion quarter horse while Dallas dismounted in one fluid, easy movement. "I trust you."

He said those words so effortlessly, and he realized once he said the words aloud that he meant it. Nick had grown to trust Dallas in a way that was rare for him. He grew up in Chicago—you had to be city savvy, and taking people at their word was a fool's mistake. He had also been raised in the "elite" class of Chicago—that was a world of lies and illusions, everyone trying to project the perfect image. Everyone lied. But not Dallas. She didn't lie. If she couldn't tell you the truth, she would go quiet. That was her way. And he really liked that about her. Yes, she was wild and unpolished and had barely gotten her GED, but she was also refreshing and fascinating and strong.

He enjoyed watching her when she ran the barrels— he enjoyed watching her while she went through the motions of caring for her horse. Nick realized, while he watched her pull her heavy saddle off the quarter horse's back, that he genuinely admired Dallas.

"What's the news?" Dallas asked him, not speaking to the fact that he had said, sincerely, that he trusted her.

He didn't expect the feeling to be mutual—not with this one.

Nick followed the cowgirl over to the spot where she always rinsed off her horse after a training session. He hung his arms over the chest-height wooden board that was the only slat left on the remnants of a fence meant to block a horse from leaving the wash area. Dallas replaced the horse's bridle with a halter and tied him down so the horse wouldn't take a walk.

"Signed, sealed and delivered," Nick said with a relieved smile. "The deal is done—Lightning Rock is officially a part of Bent Tree Ranch again."

Dallas didn't return his smile—she just gave a nod of agreement that signaled she was pleased with the outcome. When he smiled at a woman, he was used to getting the same in return. Dallas's odd response to what he had been told was an "irresistible, charming" smile took some getting used to.

"It's right." Dallas turned the water on, felt it with her hand first and then began to rinse the foamy sweat off the horse's neck and back.

"It is," Nick agreed with a shake of his head at the thought of how badly things could have gone. "Lightning Rock always belonged with Bent Tree."

The cowgirl squeegeed the excess water from the horse's coat and then sprayed him down with fly spray before she untied his lead rope.

"You managed to win in a no-win situation," Dallas said offhandedly. "Your aunt knows all the right strings to pull."

Nick knew Dallas was spot-on. Aunt Barbara had smoothed the way for him; she was the only person who could have swayed his uncle to back away from his entrenched position. He'd probably never know how she had managed to finally convince her husband to abandon his twenty-year dispute over his father's will, but Nick owed her. Big-time.

Dallas knew that the day had finally come for her to clean out her father's trailer. This was the hub of the last days of his life and she had been avoiding it. Nick, to his credit, had been following her lead on the cleanup. She decided which area of the homestead they were going to tackle. But she knew, from information she had gathered from their passing conversations, that Nick was running out of time to be in Montana. He had a job waiting for him back in Chicago—he'd been given some leeway because of his father's position at the firm, but they were about to run out of rope. She had to face the trailer. It was time.

With Nick a few feet behind her, always thoughtful and giving her some space, Dallas walked up the stairs to the trailer. Opening that door felt like an admission that Davy was truly gone. It was easy for her to just pretend that her father was holed up in this trailer, padding himself from the world with his magazines and newspapers and model cars.

Dallas's hand was still on the door handle for a couple of long minutes before she finally built the guts to turn the knob. When she opened the door, she was slapped in the face with a strong smell of paint and glue and mildew. There was so much dust in the air she could see the particles floating in front of her. She sneezed once, twice, three times in a row.

"God bless you," Nick said from his spot behind her.

Dallas sniffed several times loudly. "Wooo! It's dusty in there."

"We'll get through it." It seemed that he wanted to reassure her, to ease her embarrassment at the condition of her father's living space, and she appreciated his kindness. She'd come to rely on that kindness in a way that was not typical. Nick Brand had managed to slip into the tiniest crack in her armor. He hadn't penetrated her well-constructed armor, but he'd gotten further than most men.

Dallas untied the bandanna from around her neck and tied it over her nose and mouth before she stepped into the trailer. Everywhere she looked, there were piles and piles of papers and magazines. Her father had been a curious man—he read magazines like the *Smithsonian* and *National Geographic*. Davy Dalton also had decades of back issues of the *New York Times* and the *Wall Street Journal*. Her father had enjoyed being a rodeo man, but there was a dream he had that only his closest family and friends knew about: he had wanted to be an archaeologist from the time he was a boy. If you could get him talking, Davy could talk for hours about prehistoric man or the when and how of the construction of the pyramids. He was a walking archaeology encyclopedia.

"This is your call." Nick was standing next to her now.

"I'd like to just bulldoze the place," Dallas admitted.

It was hurtful—a mental pain that manifested as actual pain in her body—to imagine her dear father living in such a tiny, cramped space. There was only a very narrow aisle leading to the front of the trailer where the kitchen was located and the back of the trailer where

Davy spent most of his time building models of antique trucks.

They wouldn't be able to walk straight through; they would have to turn sideways and scooch both ways.

"But I can't," Dallas continued without looking at Nick. "This was Davy's bank."

She looked up at Nick then, caught, temporarily, in those clear, striking, Brand-blue eyes.

"What do you mean?" the city boy asked her.

Dallas gestured to the stacks of papers and magazines. "Davy hid his money here. And anything else he wanted to keep safe. I have no idea how much he squirreled away over the years."

Nick didn't respond to this news—he quietly looked around the space and appeared to be taking inventory and trying to gauge the work ahead.

"I can do this by myself." Dallas wanted to let the man off the hook. "Why don't you go visit your sisters or your aunt while I get this done?"

"No," Nick said with his hands resting on his hips. "I finish what I start."

Nick looked at her with that steady, calm, you-can-count-on-me look that she had come to expect. He didn't get upset or frustrated—he just picked a spot on the horizon and worked toward reaching it. It was an admirable trait and not one often found in the men she encountered who spent their lives chasing the rodeo.

One by one, they started thumbing through each magazine and newspaper, collecting money and legal documents, love letters to and from her mother, and pictures. It took them all day to clear one side of the trailer; by the end of the second day, they had managed to search through the rest of the piles.

"Twelve thousand, eight hundred and fifty dollars." Nick was sitting at the kitchen table counting the money they had found.

"Lord Almighty, Pop!" Dallas said, shocked, from her slumped position on the couch they had uncovered earlier that day.

She felt drained—physically and emotionally.

Nick sat down next to her on the couch and held out the thick stack of money. "I'd consider this to be part of your inheritance."

Dallas pushed the money away. "Give it to your uncle. He stopped chargin' Davy rent years ago. It's only fair."

"Half to you and half to your brother. You're entitled," Nick tried again.

"My brother wouldn't take a dime of Davy's money if he were dyin'."

Nick seemed to think about her response for a moment and then he counted some money out of the pile and held out the smaller of the stacks to her.

"Half for hiring some muscle to haul off this trailer and the trucks," he said. "Half to get you back to barrel racing."

Nick had been training to be a lawyer and he was going to be damn good at his job. He knew the magic words to get at her weak spot—barrel racing. She *craved* the competition. She was addicted to the nerves and the smells and the noise. She wanted her life back, and six thousand dollars would keep her afloat until she could get back to winning.

"You're sure it's mine?" She didn't take the money right away.

"I'm sure." Nick reached out for her hand and put the stack of money in it and closed her fingers over the money. "It's yours."

Dallas had decided to burn her father's stockpile of newspapers and magazines. They hauled them to the burn pile and Nick realized that when it came time to light the match, it was going to be one heck of a bonfire.

"That's the last of it." Nick took his cowboy hat, Davy's old hat, off his head and wiped the sweat from his brow.

Dallas had been a trouper throughout the entire cleanup effort. She had matched him, hour for hour, never breaking. She was tougher than any woman he'd ever met, without a doubt. There were rare moments when he saw that their work in the trailer had touched her; he had found a picture of her as a young girl, sitting on a black-and-white pinto pony, with her father standing next to her holding a trophy that was bigger than she was at the time. Dallas's eyes turned glassy with emotion when she took the picture from him and stared at it. But she didn't cry. He thought she might, but she didn't. She had tucked that picture into her back pocket and then kept right on working.

Dallas stood beside him—he'd become accustomed to the scent of her body when she'd been working all day. It was strange that he wasn't repelled by the way she smelled when she sweated. But he wasn't.

"We'll burn it tonight," Dallas said.

"All right."

"And you've already arranged to have the trucks and the trailer towed, sold or scrapped?"

"Luke gave me the name of a friend of his who could haul them off—Billy Whiteside?"

Dallas nodded that she recognized the name.

"He's coming out tomorrow to take a look and give me an estimate."

"Then we'll be done."

Nick cranked his neck around to look behind him. He couldn't believe how much work they had managed to do in such a short amount of time. He'd never worked this hard, not that he'd admit it to Dallas. He had only *thought* he knew what hard work was when he was out on his sailboat. *This* was a whole different level of labor, and it wasn't the level of labor he intended to acclimate to. His muscles were sore and stiff; dirt was ground into his hands so deep that they were gritty no matter how many times he washed them. He was tired of sleeping on a lumpy mattress that had an odor that he was unable to recognize, and he wasn't so sure he *wanted* to recognize it.

It was time to go home.

Nick could think of only one thing he wanted to do now: jump into the lake. Of all the things he had been exposed to while in Montana, most of them involving some sort of manual labor on his part, the lake was one of his pleasures. He rarely missed an opportunity to reward himself from a job well done by rinsing off the day's grime in the clear, fresh water of Sweet William Lake.

He looked over at his companion. "Are you thinking what I'm thinking?"

"I'm already there."

Nick took a minute to change into his cutoff shorts and then they walked together, side by side, not too close, and not too far away, to their mutual swimming hole. Like Dallas, Nick had grown to love this spot. The lake was fed by the melted snow that filtered down from the mountains once spring had sprung. The water was so clear that you could see to the rocks and sand at the bottom of the lake. He wore his very expensive cutoff jeans when he swam, and even though he would have preferred just to buy a bathing suit and save his designer-label jeans, he'd grown fond of the memory of Dallas lopping off his jeans to make a cowboy bathing suit.

At the lakeside now, they both started to strip off their boots, socks and shirts. Dallas always wore her modest bathing suit beneath her clothing because she always planned to swim at some point in the day. He tried not to be obvious, but he wanted to watch her disrobe.

Dallas had to recognize the interest and appreciation in his eyes when he looked at her, but she never tried to "sex it up" when she stripped off her clothes down to her bathing suit. She might have been surprised to know that for him, the fact that she didn't try to be sexy only made her sexier in his mind. Even though he had less to take off, he was always last to get undressed. This was by design. He loved to watch Dallas take her first dive off the boulder into the water. The tone of the tightly compacted muscles in her legs, the golden hue of the skin on her shoulders and arms—the wild waves of her long dark hair. She was, to his eye, a thing of beauty. A sight to behold.

She stood on the boulder, her back straight, her arms up next to her ears. She bent her knees a little and then sprang forward in a perfect arc into the air. Dallas cut through the surface of the smooth lake, making a small splash. Nick's favorite moment in this ritual was next. Dallas completely disappeared beneath the water and then a moment later she reappeared like a shot, straight up into the air, the water on her body shimmering in the sunlight.

"Are you comin' in?" Dallas called to him after she pushed the tangle of wet hair away from her face so she could open her eyes.

Nick waved his hand to indicate that he was soon to follow. He picked his way over to the boulder; he climbed on top of the hot surface of the boulder, and it registered in his brain that his feet had toughened in the short amount of time he'd been walking barefoot in Montana, because the hot rock of the boulder didn't burn the bottom of his feet quite as much as it had done in the beginning.

He gave a warning rebel yell, which was his usual. "Incoming!"

He had loved cannonballs since he was a kid and swimming in this lake reminded him of when he was a teenager visiting Montana for what turned out to be the last time. That was the visit before his grandfather had died; that was his last visit to Bent Tree for two decades.

Dallas swam away from the center of the lake so he could perform his cannonball without landing right on top of her.

He executed what he considered to be one of his biggest cannonball successes, but he waited until Dallas judged it.

When he came up to the surface, he wiped the water off his face and sought out the cowgirl. On the bank of the lake, Dallas was holding up her arms and displaying ten fingers.

"Ten!" she shouted loudly.

Nick hit the water with his hands. "I *knew* it was my best. I *felt* it!"

They took turns diving off the boulder—they swam laps, they floated. They allowed themselves the luxury of relaxing now that the bulk of their job was completed and behind them. Now drying off on the boulder, sitting close, but as always not *too* close, Nick was flat on his back, hands behind his head, eyes closed and soaking up the midafternoon sun.

"Life is good," he murmured tiredly.

"Uh-huh."

"How soon do you think you'll be heading out after we're done?"

"Um. There's a pro-sanctioned rodeo in Livingston—if I can catch that one, I will. Then I'll head over to Wolfpoint, Montana. After that—I don't know—I could catch another in Montana, but I might head out to Colorado."

Nick opened his eyes and looked over at the woman sitting cross-legged next to him. She had her eyes open and she was staring straight ahead to the mountains in the distance.

"Wherever the wind blows?" he asked her.

She turned her face toward him and gave him the faintest of smiles. "Uh-uh."

Nick couldn't imagine living his life like that anymore; he'd lived that way in his twenties, but he wouldn't want to live like that again. Basically, untethered. He liked having a place to go to work—he liked having his condo in a building that had concierge. He liked having a schedule and consistency. The kind of life Dallas chose to live, while it sounded free and loose, wasn't the way of life he wanted anymore. She seemed to thrive on it.

When it was time to leave, Nick offered his hand to Dallas out of habit to help her down from the boulder. Normally, she ignored that hand. Today, for the first time, she took it and jumped lightly to the ground.

"I want to thank you," Dallas said after she got dressed. "You being here made all this a lot easier on me."

Nick smiled down at her. "I was happy to do it, Dallas. I was glad to help you. I was glad to honor the memory of Davy Dalton."

On a whim, Nick leaned down and plucked a small bundle of Sweet William from the ground and handed them to Dallas. "For you."

Nick was relieved when the prickly cowgirl accepted his offer of friendship in the form of her favorite wildflowers. Dallas smiled that little smile again, so faint it was hard to catch, as she brought the bundle of Sweet William up to her nose. They walked back to the homestead, and it seemed a quieter walk, perhaps because they both knew that this would be one of their last swims together in the lake. Nick didn't want to read too much into Dallas's actions, because after all, when would he see her again? He waited for her to throw those flowers away along the path back to the homestead. Yet she didn't. And the fact that she didn't throw those flowers away meant more to him than it probably should have. That much he did know.

Chapter Six

The trailer was hauled away first. And then, one by one, each of Davy's antique trucks was pulled onto a flatbed to be taken away. Of all the things that seemed to impact Dallas the most, watching those trucks being dislodged from their resting place brought her to tears. It hit her out of the blue—she had already cried for her father in private. In her mind, that should have sufficed. In her experience, tears were never a solution to any of her problems.

"Are you okay?" Nick asked her.

Dallas rubbed the tears from her eyes and off her cheeks; she pinched her nose to stop the tears, but they came, unchecked, anyway. She wanted to tell Nick that she was fine, but she couldn't seem to get the words out.

Nick put one arm around the back of her shoulders and the other arm around the front of her body. He locked his fingers together and hugged her into his body. It felt good to have someone to hug when she was saying a final goodbye to her father. It felt good to have a friend like Nick who had never expected anything from her—he had only offered her help without ever asking for something in return. So, in that specific moment in time, she gladly accepted the comfort he was offering because she knew that it came without any strings attached.

Together, they watched as the last, the best, of Davy's antique trucks was pulled onto the flatbed.

"That's the one that breaks my heart," Nick said quietly about the last truck.

"That was Pop's favorite." Dallas signaled that she wanted to be let go and Nick's arms immediately fell away. "It makes me feel…"

Nick looked at her, waiting for her next words. But she still couldn't put words to how all this made her feel. The feeling that was scratching its way to the top through the layer of sorrow? Fury. She was *furious* with her father for never restoring the truck like he promised he would. She was *furious* with her father for letting that beautiful antique turn into a barely recognizable hunk of junk that had to be pulled out of the weeds with a heavy chain and a crank. How could he have wasted his life? How could he have put all his time and energy into collecting those stupid papers and magazines?

She would never truly understand it—not as long as she lived. Dallas tucked her hands into the back pockets of her jeans.

"Well," she said to her city boy. "That's that."

"That's that," Nick answered with his eyes still on the flatbed of 1950s trucks being hauled away.

Dallas held out her hand to Nick. "Again—I can't thank you enough."

Nick noticed her offered hand after the trucks disappeared from sight. He frowned at her, his arms stretched out in question. "Really? A handshake?"

Dallas's smile was a little wider, a little more genuine when she titled her head back so she could see his eyes beyond the rim of her cowgirl hat.

Nick did take her hand, but he used it to pull her into his arms. He gave her a real bear hug: strong, tight and full of feeling.

After the hug, respectful of her space as he always was, Nick stepped back and gave her some room.

"When do you head back home?" she asked him as they walked slowly to his rental car already packed with his belongings.

"Saturday."

That was four days away and then Nick Brand would be going back to his life and she would already have returned to hers. She had the distinct feeling that waking up tomorrow without Nick would be more impactful than she was willing to acknowledge. She had become accustomed to having him around. Nick had found a spot inside of her heart.

Nick paused by the rental car. "I have some visiting to do with my sisters before I leave. They're planning another family dinner out at Bent Tree."

"Uh-huh." She kept her hands in her back pockets to stop herself from reaching out and straightening the collar of his shirt.

"You aren't going to still be in town Friday night, will you?"

"No." She shook her head. "I'll already be on the road."

"I was thinking that you could join us Friday if you were still going to be in town." Nick seemed to be stalling his departure. "Aunt Barb would be happy to have you."

"I'll already be gone," she reiterated. Lingering around, drawing out goodbyes wasn't in her DNA. She liked to yank that Band-Aid off and get on with it. Life was rolling on whether she dragged her feet or not.

Nick nodded in what she interpreted as acceptance as he opened the driver's door.

"Are you sure you want me to keep this?" he asked about the cowboy hat he had just taken off his head.

"Davy would be proud for you to have it."

With that, Nick got into the car and cranked the engine. They said another goodbye and promised to keep in touch through text and social media. She always posted pictures on social media, as did he, so it was a good way to keep in touch.

Dallas watched as Nick Brand drove away; yes, she would see him on social media, but would she ever see him in person again? It was hard to imagine a time when their paths would cross. He had his life in Chicago, and she had her life as a traveling barrel racer. And now that Davy's affairs were put in order, she could get back to that life.

"Well, Dally," she scolded herself aloud when she was still looking at the empty road long after Nick's car had disappeared. "Pick up your lip and get on with it already."

Nick had been back in Chicago for a month and he had returned to the blessed routine of his city life. He had gotten a much-needed haircut and a professional shave; he'd managed to scrub the feeling of grit and dirt off his body with the help of his high-tech, state-of-the-art shower with multiple showerheads. His back had finally stopped aching after regular massages and the benefit of his top-of-the-line mattress. The bug bites, the scrapes, the bruises had healed as the weeks passed. The new job was going well—he had always been a staff favorite when he visited his father at the firm— now that he had passed the bar exam, he fit into the conservative, high-priced culture of the firm. It was, indeed, good to be Nick Brand.

There was just one small fly in the ointment: Dallas Dalton.

Damn it if he didn't genuinely miss that hard-to-figure-out, wild-child cowgirl. He really did. He didn't miss Lightning Rock and he sure as heck didn't miss that horrible shack and prison cot, but he did miss Dallas. When he was out on a date with a woman, he caught himself naturally comparing her with Dallas; so far, his dates, as lovely and as elegant, educated and suitable as they were, had not measured up to the cowgirl. There was something that she had on the inside of her—something about her heart, her honesty and her refusal to live life any other way than *her* way. She had the focus and determination that a lot of men in positions of power would pay big money to learn how to get.

Dallas impressed him. Dallas intrigued him. Dallas made him feel something in his gut that was strange and new. And after a month of texting back and forth, catching up with quickie conversations and stalking her on social media, Nick decided that he had to try to break free of the "friend zone." He needed to do something big—something that would get Dallas's attention. From her last text, he knew that she was on her way to Texas after hitting all the pro rodeos in Montana. He booked a flight to Fort Worth; his surprise appearance at her next rodeo would either freak her out and force her to unfriend him on social media *or* she would be excited to see him and their relationship could have a chance of going to the next level. Although he wasn't really sure what a next level would look like with Dallas. She was so darn prickly—she had such a tough exterior—what would she do if he tried to lean over and steal a kiss? He really didn't have an answer to that, and he had to admit that *not knowing* was part of the fun of hanging out with Dallas Dalton.

"Nice run, Dally!" one of her fellow barrel racers called out to her as she walked back to where she had parked her trailer.

"I sliced the third on the way out," Dallas called back. She'd had a hard time getting back into the swing of her life after Lightning Rock. She'd been slow out of the chute and she'd been sloppy around the barrels.

Ever since Lightning Rock, she'd been off her game. She'd been distracted and she was never distracted! Nick was never far from her mind—when she was driving, when she was getting ready to ride—she seemed to always have Nick Brand on the brain. She had worked for years to insulate herself from relationships so she could concentrate on her career without distractions. And then came Nick.

"You'll get it next round!" The barrel racer called back to her.

Maybe she would; maybe she wouldn't.

She been chasing the big money and the big endorsements for a lot of years. Perhaps it was time to admit that she needed a different game plan. Now that her sometimes travel partner and full-time rodeo support, Clint, was retiring from the rodeo so he could stay home with his wife and daughter, her old way of hitting rodeos wasn't going to work. She needed to work smarter, drive fewer miles, save her strength and Blue's legs. She made some mistakes, but she had finished in the money more often than not. If she got back on her game, she'd still qualify for the National Final Rodeo in Las Vegas.

"I'm always amazed at how aggressive you are out there." A male voice pulled her out of her own head. "I love to watch you work."

Nick Brand, dressed in his crisp Chicago casual clothing, was leaning against her busted Bronco waiting for her.

"What on God's green earth are you doin' in Texas?" Dallas's heart gave a little jump at the sight of the man who had dominated her thoughts. He was the last person she'd expect to find at a rodeo in Fort Worth. But he was the person she had wanted to see the most.

"You're in Texas." He replied with that smile she had missed.

Nick looked at her like he always did—open, friendly, interested. He liked her. It never occurred to her that he liked her enough to come find her in a less-than-glamorous town in Texas.

She opened the door to the storage area of her trailer with her heavy saddle balanced on her hip and Blue's bridle hung over her shoulder. Silently, with her mind whirling with questions, she put up her tack. Once she was done, and it only took a moment, she stopped right in front of her surprise visitor.

"Hi." Nick looked down at her with a smile that reached those spectacular blue eyes of his. Undoubtedly, those bright Brand-blue eyes were the feature that hooked her.

"Hi there." He looked happy to see her and she *felt* happy to see him.

Nick had gotten to her—he really had—and that didn't happen very often for her. She'd spent her life with rodeo men, cowboys, and bull riders and ranchers. She was friends with these men; she loved their spirit and their toughness. But she had always wanted different for herself. She didn't want to marry a cowboy. If she married at all, she wanted to marry someone who could show her new slices of life. That desire was the thing that made it easy for her to stay focused on her first love: barrel racing.

"Where's Blue?"

"I got him bedded down for the day—we get assigned stalls when we punch in."

Nick crossed his arms loosely in front of his body as he said, "You know, I'm still not sure what I'm supposed to be looking for, but I know you're running against the clock." He sounded impressed. "You were fast."

"I was fast," Dallas agreed with an irritated tone in her voice. "But I sliced the third barrel and took myself right out of the money."

"You looked like a million bucks to my eyes," Nick said with a nonchalant shrug. When she thanked him for the compliment, it was genuine. It was nice to have an outsider appreciate the whole picture instead of nitpicking her performance to death like she would. That little clip of the third barrel would keep her up half the night wondering how she could have avoided it; it wasn't Blue's fault—he was such a good, hardworking mount. It was her mistake, her misjudgment.

Dallas took a break from the conversation to get her gear set up for the next day of competition; once she was satisfied that she hadn't missed anything, she left the tiny mobile tack room.

"I'm glad to see you." She hooked her thumb on her pocket.

"I'm glad to see you too."

"I'm just surprised to see you here, is all." She said the statement like a question.

"I just wanted to see you." That was his simple answer to the hesitation in her voice. "That's all there is to it. I wanted to see you."

"You flew to Texas," Dallas pointed out.

"That's true."

"You must've wanted to see me pretty bad."

Nick laughed. "That's also true."

"How long were you plannin' on stayin'?"

She'd never had anyone go this out of their way for her—not even Clint. It made her feel special—and nervous all at the same time.

"Just overnight. I fly out tomorrow." Nick was back to leaning against her trailer.

Looking into his handsome face made her stomach flip-flop. Nick Brand hadn't flown all the way to Texas to get her into bed. She had a pit in her stomach that told her that Nick might want something much more intimate than just plain sex. And this inkling made her more nervous, and more skittish, than any regular ol' sexual pass ever would.

"I was hoping…" Nick sought out her eyes as he continued "…that you would have dinner with me tonight."

She was so disarmed by his simple invitation, wrapped up in an incredible surprise visit at her rodeo.

"All right," Dallas said with a nod.

"All right?" He repeated her response as a question as if he didn't believe her the first time.

This small sliver of insecurity in a man who always seemed to be perfectly secure made her smile at him. "I'd like to. Yes."

The idea of sharing a meal with Nick instead of spending the night alone, mentally rewinding and reviewing her mistakes in her head, sounded like the best alternative option she'd had in a long, long while.

"We could eat here, if you have the kind of stomach that can handle greasier-the-better rodeo food."

"I have a room at the Omni downtown." Nick pushed away from the trailer and took a step toward her. "Their steak house is supposed to be one of the best in Fort Worth. How does that sound?"

A thick, juicy steak *or* the stale ham sandwich she had leftover from lunch? "Like a good idea."

She had agreed to meet him at the hotel for an early dinner. He waited for her at the entrance of the hotel—he had offered to go back to the rodeo and pick her up, but in typical Dallas fashion, she insisted on driving herself. Dallas's beat-up Bronco, in serious need of a tune-up and a new muffler, did not fit with the swanky downtown Omni. When he saw the Bronco pull up to the front of his hotel, it struck him how far apart their worlds really were. This was the first time he'd seen Dallas outside her surroundings; this was the first time she was seeing Nick in what was more *his* natural environment. There were a couple of very lengthy seconds when he wondered if this spontaneous trip to Fort Worth, and this dinner invitation, was a terrible idea.

But then he saw her walking toward him, her dark hair, long and wispy and blowing around her shoulders. She was wearing dark jeans and a silky Western-style long-sleeve shirt with a pair of dressy cowgirl boots. He saw her and the doubt evaporated into the balmy night air.

Nick offered her his arm. "I have to say, you look mighty pretty tonight, Ms. Dalton."

"You look like you did the first day I met you."

Nick felt like a proud man escorting Dallas into the Omni—as was always the case with the cowgirl, men noticed her. She had a confidence in her walk, and an independence in her eyes, that was just as appealing as a pair of super long legs, blond hair and cleavage.

Dallas looked everywhere while they walked together through the lobby to Bob's Steak House. Nick's reservations were confirmed by the hostess and they were escorted to their table.

"This is some swanky motel." Dallas sat down across the table from him.

"It's nice," Nick agreed. It was far from the most elegant hotel he'd stayed in, but his suite was roomy and the office space was separate from the bedroom in case he needed to work.

Water was poured and menus were delivered.

"Would you like me to order wine?" Nick asked, realizing that he didn't even know if Dallas drank alcohol. He'd never seen her indulge.

"I'd really like a beer," she said. "Something on tap."

Nick put the wine list away in favor of ordering them both a beer on tap. They placed their orders, both opting to go with a porterhouse steak, and then Nick offered his beer glass up for a toast. "Here's to…"

"Qualifying for the NFR." Dallas finished the toast as his pause had encouraged.

"I don't know what that is, but I'll toast to it." Nick tapped his glass to hers and then took a healthy drink of his beer. It was cold and hit the spot. A beer, as it turned out, was a better idea than wine.

"The National Finals Rodeo—it's the mack daddy of all rodeos. Big money, endorsements. That's what everyone's after whether they're willin' to admit it out loud or not."

Nick liked to hear Dallas talk about her passion; the more she talked about barrel racing, the more he got to catch glimpses of that sweet, fleeting smile of hers. Whenever she was done talking about one aspect of her sport, he asked her another question just to keep her from winding down.

After their plates were cleared away, Dallas said, "All I've done is talk about me and my stuff the whole time."

"I'm not complaining." Nick drank some water. "I like to listen to you talk."

Dallas looked away from him as if his comment had made her feel self-conscious. Then she looked back at him. "It's been real tough bein' out here on the road without Clint."

Nick knew that Clint was married to his sister; he also knew that Clint and Dallas had never been more than friends. And yet it still bothered him to hear how much Dallas missed having Clint on the rodeo circuit with her. Maybe it was because he knew how much Dallas trusted Clint and he wanted her to trust *him* that way.

"I really wanted to talk to him tonight—tell him about what happened out there today. He could always get me out of my own head, you know? But he's married. He's got a baby. I can't call him every time I have a bad day."

Dallas looked at him directly in his eyes—completely unguarded for a moment or two as she continued, "I really needed someone to talk to tonight, Nick."

After dinner, Nick walked Dallas back to her Bronco. They both needed to get back to their separate lives the next day.

"Thank you for joining me for dinner," Nick said as they reached her vehicle.

"I want to thank you." Dallas smiled up at him in the moonlight. "I'm stuffed to the gills. I'm all talked out. I think I'm gonna sleep just like a baby."

"I'm glad."

They stared at each other for several silent seconds before Dallas reached to open the driver's door.

"Dallas?"

"Hmm?"

As the cowgirl turned back toward him, Nick put his hands on either side of her face and gave the cowgirl a very gentle, totally unassuming, yet firm enough to be memorable, lover's first kiss.

Chapter Seven

Dallas had to admit that, after Nick's visit, she was in a considerably better mood. The loneliness void she had been feeling for her friend Clint had been filled, at least in part, by Nick's visit. To have someone fly in to town to surprise her, just because he wanted to see her, was an amazing thing. It truly was. And she was flattered. Flattered by the thought behind the visit; flattered that someone like Nick—handsome, educated, well bred, well traveled—had seen something interesting in her. Interesting enough to hop on a plane and come to Fort Worth.

She wasn't one to have a crush; maybe some things that happened early on in her life had blocked her from developing crushes. Just like Dorothy in *The Wizard of Oz*, once the curtain was pulled back, she'd never again believe that the wizard was "great and wonderful."

It was rare that she let herself count on someone in her life—she learned much too young to be self-sufficient. At Lightning Rock, she had started to count on Nick. Not for anything tangible—not for anything material—

she had begun to count on his nature. He was good-natured. He wasn't prone to temper flare-ups. Nick was goal oriented, supportive, considerate and kind. These were rare qualities miraculously bundled into one man. And he was not a cowboy. He was "other than" the men she was surrounded by day in and day out. Did she see herself with Nick Brand as a long-term gig? She wasn't all that certain she saw herself with *anyone* in that capacity. But, she had to admit that she was smitten with Nick. It was just a fact. She had pressed the wildflowers he had given her back at Lightning Rock into the pages of one of her prized equine medicine books; she looked at that dried little bundle of Sweet William wildflowers often. And the kiss. That sweet, gentle, "let's take it one step at a time, I'm not going to push you," first kiss had been perfect. For her.

After a disappointing show at Fort Worth, Dallas packed up her gear, loaded Blue into her trailer and set a course for San Antonio. She knew the roads well, and for the most part she liked traveling on her own. Many of the other barrel racers would travel together or they had a spouse, friends or assistants travel with them. Clint was the only person she ever traveled with, and that wasn't all the time. No—she liked the freedom of traveling by herself. It was lonely, but that was also the life she had dreamt about, way back when she was a "barrel racing sensation" as a preteenager.

"You were fast *and* you didn't slice any of the barrels this time."

Nick!

They had been talking on the phone all throughout the week, even if it was just to catch up for a couple of quick minutes, and he had never mentioned that he was even thinking about meeting her in San Antonio. She was completely surprised again, and completely pleased, to see him waiting for her directly outside the exhibitor exit gate.

"See?" He smiled at her with that charming smile of his. "I'm learning."

There it was again—that flip-flop her heart did every time she saw Nick.

"Welcome to San Antonio." This was said with a small but happy smile.

Dallas swung out of the saddle and officially greeted Nick with a long, hard hug.

"Man, do I love to watch you ride!" Nick fell in beside her as she walked Blue back to his temporary stall.

"Why?" She laughed, still pleased that he was with her again.

"I don't know how to explain it," Nick replied. "I can't take my eyes off you."

He hung out with her while she tended to Blue, and it seemed to her that he was patiently awaiting his turn for her attention.

The last item in her post-run ritual was to kiss Blue on the spot on his nose before she gave him a pad of his favorite hay.

"Do I get one of those too?" Nick asked her.

Dallas gave him a quick peck on the cheek, but Nick held on to her hand and reeled her back in toward him. He kissed her on the lips—undemanding, simple, honest—a second perfect kiss.

"Hi," Nick said after the kiss.

"Hi." She loved the feel of his lips on hers.

"Do you know what occurred to me yesterday?"

She shook her head, caught up in his ocean-blue eyes.

"I hadn't asked you out on a second date."

"That is true."

Nick reached for her hand and she didn't have her normal, knee-jerk response when someone touched her without warning—she didn't pull away from him.

"Would you go out with me tonight, Dallas?"

Dallas pretended to think longer than she needed. "I suppose I can make room on my social calendar."

Nick took her to a downtown nightspot in San Antonio, Deep Ellum, where the small beer brewery reigned supreme. It was a Saturday night and downtown San Antonio was bustling and buzzing with college students and San Antonio young professionals and tourists alike. The sidewalks in the Deep Ellum area were jammed, and Dallas was happy to hold on to Nick's hand to keep from being separated from him.

"I've already scoped out some microbreweries for us to try." Nick had an excited gleam in his eye and an energy in his body that he simply didn't have in the mountains of Montana.

He thrived in a city like San Antonio—this was the most liberal and cosmopolitan city in Texas and it was dominated by students from the University of Texas at San Antonio, where one of their buildings was so big that it needed its own zip code. Unlike in Lightning Rock, where she was in her element and often led the way, tonight she was following Nick's lead.

"I have to compete tomorrow," she reminded him.

"We're going to sample—not chug," Nick reassured her. "Don't worry. I'll make sure you get home safe and are in good shape to kick ass tomorrow."

They started at the Deep Ellum Brewing Company

and then just hopped from one microbrewery to the next, sharing a mug of beer, often only taking a couple of sips before they were on to the next stop on the tour Nick had planned for them. Dallas loved walking with Nick, holding his hand—women noticed this man. It was in the way he held himself, the cut and quality of his business-casual clothing—his manners. Yes, he was a handsome man in his own right; he had a strong nose, a strong jawline. He had an alpha male aura that other men seemed to acknowledge. And she was the lucky woman on his arm.

Nick had remembered that Dallas had ordered a beer instead of wine on their first date, so he thought that a great second date would be to take her on his own personal tour of San Antonio's microbreweries. The side benefit? It was a great excuse to hold her hand. Nick, like most men, had an eye for attractive women. And there were *many* young, sexy women all over Deep Ellum on a Saturday night. Yet, unlike when he was out on dates with other women, he didn't have to work to keep his attention on Dallas. She was a magnet for his eyes.

"So, how do you think our second date is going?"

He didn't usually fish for compliments, but he wanted Dallas to like being with him and it was hard to read her signals. Yes, she was smiling more than she did when they were together at Lightning Rock; but he didn't consider that a good benchmark, because their job at Lightning Rock had been such a somber one—it would be a really bad sign if she weren't smiling more now.

"I guess it's goin' fine." Dallas's eyes had been floating around the room, but she brought them back to his face to answer his question.

"Fine?" he asked her with feigned shock and hurt. *"Fine?"*

"I didn't mean I was havin' a bad time," his date clarified.

"Oh!" Nick rolled his eyes dramatically. "That's heartening to know."

That made Dallas laugh, which was like winning a jackpot for Nick. He loved to hear her laugh. When she laughed, it made him want to laugh along with her.

The cowgirl reached out, grabbed his hand and shook it a couple of times. "Quit twistin' my words, Nick! I meant that I don't have much to compare it to. I don't go out on dates all that often."

"I'm sure that's not for a lack of asking." Nick took a sip of the beer they were sharing.

Nick remembered how much attention Dallas's barrel practice had drawn from the cowboys on his uncle's ranch. He'd also seen how much attention Dallas got from the men at these rodeos. The interest was there, if only one-sided.

"I get asked." Dallas fiddled with the small cross on a gold chain hanging around her neck. "Not as much anymore. I've said no to just about everyone who's wanted to ask."

Nick processed that information, and once it registered it made him feel better about his grand gestures of catching a plane and flying to Texas.

He took her hand in his. "You said yes to me. Twice."

"I know." Dallas seemed surprised at her own willingness to say yes to him.

"Man, it's taking me every ounce of my self-control

and pride not to ask you why you said no to so many cowboys and yes to an attorney from Chicago," Nick said, only half kidding. He really did want to know. Was this an experiment, or was she feeling the same special chemistry between them that he was?

He decided to ask anyway. "Why'd you say yes to me, Dallas?" This time, he had a serious bent to his question.

"You have nice manners," the cowgirl answered with that honesty he admired. "And kind eyes."

Nick wanted to kiss her right there in front of all the microbrewery patrons; he held his ardor because he knew that Dallas wouldn't want to be kissed out in the open where they were. She was more private about her business. He'd never been all that private, but about his impromptu visits to Texas he hadn't breathed a word to his family, his friends, his coworkers or on social media. And he had to admit that he was glad that Dallas, who was open on social media about her barrel racing experiences, hadn't shared one post about their first date.

"Do you have any idea how much I like you, Ms. Dalton?"

"Not really." Another honest response. "But it must be a whole heck of a lot for you to come all the way out to Texas two weekends in a row."

They found a street vendor that looked semitrustworthy and tried to sop up some of the alcohol in their systems eating frankfurters with the works, hold the onions. The clock was working against him, and he knew it. The nightlife in Deep Ellum was winding up when it was time for Dallas to start winding down. They passed several of Dallas's contemporaries on the sidewalk, but Nick was more than aware of the cowgirl's ambitions. He loved her goal-oriented nature, he admired it, but it didn't help his chances of keeping her out longer on this date.

"I've got to get you back," Nick said as they stood on a street corner in Deep Ellum.

Everything about that night had been working in his favor—the Texas late-summer evening was warm but not humid, the sky was clear, and the microbrewery district was brimming with energy and activity. People were happy in Deep Ellum; with Dallas at his side, he was one of those happy people.

Nick hailed a cab and gave the driver the directions. In the back of the cab, they were both quiet but sat close together, their hands clasped.

"I'll be just a minute," Nick told the cabby when they stopped.

Holding on to Dallas's hand, he walked with her back to her trailer. In the dim light cast off by the campground lighting, Nick pulled the cowgirl into his arms. He hugged her, not wanting to let her go this time. "I've got this huge suite back at the Omni with a second bed that you could use. I feel like a real jerk dropping you off here."

"This is what I'm used to." Dallas brushed away his concern. "I have everything I need here—a bed, a shower, a fridge."

"You know I wouldn't try to talk you into anything you weren't ready to do." Nick had his hands on the top of her muscular arms. "That's not why I offered."

"I know. But I like to keep my edge. I can't always stay in motels, and I sure as heck can't stay in hotels like the Omni. No sense getting used to something I can't have."

Nick brought one of his hands up to her face. Such a pretty face—her cheekbones, her lips.

"Is it a mistake for me to get used to seeing you?" he asked her.

She hesitated to answer, so he stopped the next words from coming out her mouth by kissing them away.

Each kiss was a little bit deeper, a little bit longer, a little bit more sensual. This time, he lingered on her lips, tasting her, feeling her, while his arms held her more closely to his body. He wanted more, but the moment he felt her tense, the second he felt her resist, he ended the kiss and let her go.

"I have to get some sleep," she said, her hand resting on his chest.

Was she keeping her at arm's length with that hand? Was she resting that hand over his heart deliberately?

With this second date, he had more questions than answers about his relationship with this enigmatic rodeo girl.

"Thank you, Nick." Dallas's hand fell away from him. "For the best date I've ever had."

Dallas left San Antonio on an upswing, emotionally and professionally. She had great rounds, Blue was in top shape and she had done her job to support her horse around the barrels. Her next and last stop was Houston and then she was going to head back to Montana to give Blue a well-deserved rest from the road and competition. Many of the rodeos sanctioned by the Women's Professional Rodeo Association were in Montana, so she could rest up and then get back to it without much driving.

On the drive from San Antonio to Houston, she wondered if Nick was going to surprise her again. The rodeo was several weeks away and she was going to be parking on a friend's land just outside Houston, where she could turn Blue out to graze and keep the barrel racer's endurance high between competitions. The thought of seeing Nick again excited her in a way that felt odd and foreign. Much like their last kiss. She had kept men in the friend zone for so long—she had focused on her career for so long—all this slow-burning romance with Nick felt fresh and brand-new.

On her downtime before the next competition, Dallas spoke with Nick several times a week, and they texted regularly every day. He was always so busy with his new job at the law firm and catching up with his friends, whom he'd blown off two weekends in a row. The things that he liked to do on his downtime weren't her idea of a good time—she didn't understand why he liked to spend time at his country club golfing, she didn't understand the attraction of taking a boat out onto the water, parking it for a while and then taking it back to the dock. She wasn't really a water person, other than swimming in small lakes like Sweet William, but Nick liked boating on Lake Michigan—one of the most dangerous of the Great Lakes. Lake Michigan was too big and too busy and too treacherous for her liking. Yes, she was an adrenaline junky, but she liked to get her adrenaline rushes while on dry land.

It was in her downtime, thinking about Nick in Chicago, living in his state-of-the-art, best-of-everything, high-rise condo with his fancy country club friends, when she really started to question their relationship. No, they hadn't crossed any serious boundaries. They were dating but hadn't made any promises. Nick was free to date while he was in Chicago, and she was just as free to date while she was living her life on the road.

In her mind, whenever she imagined herself in a serious relationship, it was never with a cowboy. Nick treated her like a lady—he was raised with old-school manners, he was a gentleman and she loved it. He was like his uncle Hank in that way, and it made sense—they were all Brands. Nick was a city Brand, but a Brand nonetheless. When she was out with him, he knew how to order, he taught her about food, and she loved to listen to his stories about his travels in Europe and Asia and the Middle East.

The attraction was real. The mutual interest was real. But was it sustainable? Doubtful. Highly doubtful. Would that stop her from going out with him again or kissing him again? Doubtful. Highly doubtful.

The week leading up to the Houston rodeo, Nick had been preparing her for the fact that he couldn't get away. He hadn't said it directly, but he had been wrapped up in his first big case for the firm and he needed to spend late nights at the office and spend the weekends working. Part of her thought that he was trying to get her off the scent; on the other hand, he had an important job to do and his father's reputation at the firm to uphold. Either way, her downtime was over and it was time for her to get her head back into her own game. Nick was a distraction; he was a very wonderful, funny, handsome distraction, but still a distraction.

The Houston rodeo offered an indoor venue, which was one of the reasons she selected it. The money was decent, but the experience Blue would get running barrels indoors was invaluable. Horses always reacted differently running barrels inside versus how they would run in an outdoor arena. The NFR in Las Vegas? Indoor, all the way.

Dallas was dressed in her competition garb, and Blue was tacked up in his show bridle and show saddle, his legs were wrapped and ready to go, and they were in the line of competitors, waiting their turn to race. Many of the horses were anxious, pacing, moving back and forth, dancing to the side, tossing their heads, and champing at their bits. Some of the riders needed a handler at the horse's head to get it moving forward. Blue was always calmer than the other horses, which sometimes put Dallas at a disadvantage at the jump. With all the nervous energy coming off the riders and the horses, she had to fight to keep her mind focused on the barrels instead of absorbing all the anxiety crackling in the air around her.

The line kept moving; barrel racing was a speed sport. One by one, the riders in front of her ran their race.

"Okay, boy," Dallas said, loud enough for Blue to hear her over the din around them. "It's time to go to work."

The horse in front of them, a huge, gorgeous dappled gray, was fighting the bit, trying to bound forward, rearing up again and again. Barrel racing horses could get sour and act out before they raced. They knew they were about to be asked to go from stop to full steam ahead. If Blue started to act like this in the chute, Dallas would retire him hands down.

The dappled gray shot out of the chute and the rider had a solid run. A real solid run. Blue started prancing, and the moment she got the signal she let her steed have his head and they started to gallop through the long track out to the arena. Her race around the barrels always happened so quick that it felt like a flash. She couldn't hear the crowd; she didn't notice them. All she saw was the barrels. All she felt was the strength and balance of the horse beneath her. If she did her job, she'd work with Blue to curve around those barrels without touching them and get up in the stirrups so he could gallop full speed to the end of the coarse.

In the span of a couple of seconds, her run was over. She galloped through the long chute out of the arena used to give the horse and rider a chance to ease out of the full-throttle run.

Blue slowed to a trot and Dallas patted him on his neck to praise him. They'd worked out there just as they should. Her time was solid and she hadn't touched the barrels. She had a shot at the money and being advanced to the next round.

"Good boy!" Dallas gave the quarter horse his head on a long rein. "Good boy!"

She left the arena feeling like she was on a cloud. Her trip to Texas had been a series of professional ups and downs. Blue had always done his part, but she hadn't always been able to do hers.

"You! Are! In-*credible*!"

That cherry on top of that amazing run—perhaps the best run of her trip to Texas—was seeing Nick Brand waiting for her outside the arena wearing her father's favorite cowboy hat and holding a small bunch of Montana wildflowers in his hand. Heaven.

Chapter Eight

Dallas couldn't wait to get off Blue Holiday and get into Nick's arms.

"You're here!" She hugged him so hard that the muscles in her arms started to shake.

"That was way too long between dates." Nick picked her up off the ground and hugged her back just as hard.

"I had these sent from Montana just for you." He held out the bouquet of wildflowers out to her.

Moved by the sweet gesture, Dallas accepted the flowers and rewarded Nick with the quickest kiss on the lips. It was the first kiss she had initiated; she doubted the recipient had any clue how significant that one little gesture was for her.

"I'm so happy you're here!" She knew her face must be beaming with happiness from her wonderful run and the excitement of seeing him again.

"I was trying pretty hard to convince you that I wasn't going to be able to make it." He walked beside her as she headed back to long rows of tents turned temporary stalls. "Are you really all that surprised?"

"Pleasantly."

Nick seemed to be as happy to see her as she was him. They didn't make a whole lot of sense on paper—they really didn't. But did that matter when just being near each other was a source of happiness? Did it matter that they were different on just about every level when their hearts seemed to be so similar?

He asked her, so gentlemanly, for a third date. This time, she said yes with a condition—they had to wait until she was done with her competing the next day. It wasn't Nick's fault, but her focus hadn't been what it should have been in Fort Worth or in San Antonio. Houston was her last chance to finish high in the money and ride a wave of success back to the competitions scheduled throughout Montana.

"Tomorrow, then," Nick said before he leaned over and touched his lips to hers. He promised to watch her compete from the stands, cheering her on. "We'll celebrate."

Nick spent the morning enjoying room service in his luxury suite at the Four Seasons Houston. He checked and answered his work emails, glad that he could keep in touch without letting anyone know where he was for the weekend. He still didn't know what he was doing with Dallas Dalton—he still didn't know how to explain what he was feeling to his friends, his parents and his colleagues. He did know something with a high level of certainty: Dallas would not fit as easily into his life as he had with hers. He could sit in the stands surrounded by cowboy hats, Wrangler jeans, silver belt buckles and cowboy boots and no one really cared that he was dressed in "preppy" clothes. He liked his chinos, button-down shirts and stylish men's shoes. He'd always been a good dresser and he could keep on wearing his "uniform" in Houston, San Antonio and Fort Worth. On the other hand, Dallas wearing her cowgirl clothes at his country club? His mother would have an epic meltdown, which would prove to be annoying and inconvenient.

But in the end, he was a grown-ass man; he would date whomever he wished. He just needed to get his sea legs with this relationship first and then figure out a game plan to ease Dallas into his life.

"Are we all set for tonight?" Nick asked the concierge on his way to watch Dallas in her last day of competition.

"All set, Mr. Brand. I've booked you for two in the Cellar private dining room. Per your request, it's the most romantic dining we offer."

Nick slipped the concierge a neatly folded one-hundred-dollar bill and then waited for valet parking to bring the Porsche he had rented to the front of the hotel. He arrived at the rodeo just in time to catch the beginning of the women's barrel racing.

He managed to find a decent seat where he could watch out for Dallas. There were a lot of really good barrel racers at this rodeo, but he only had eyes for Dallas. When he heard her named, the nerve endings in his body lit up like Christmas morning. He leaned forward, his hands clasped, all his visual attention aimed at the opening at one end of the arena where he knew that, any moment, Dallas and Blue would come flying out at a full gallop.

Man, did he want her to have a great race! The moment she came out into the arena, and the announcer mentioned that she was Davy Dalton's daughter, the crowd cheered louder for her than they did for any of the other women. Davy Dalton was still a fan favorite, and Nick was proud to be the man who would be leaving the rodeo with Davy's daughter on his arm.

"Come on, Dally." Nick clasped his hands tightly in suspense while Dallas cut around the first barrel without clipping it.

Blue was running fast and tight, his footing solid on the turns. Dallas, unlike many of the women, rode close to the saddle throughout her run and seemed to be in total control of her body.

God, she was a beautiful thing to behold when she was racing the barrels. Just as much as the first day he had caught sight of her riding Blue, he was fascinated now. Maybe even more so.

When Dallas rounded the last barrel, free and clear, she leaned forward and gave Blue his head and they took off at a full gallop to the end of the course. Nick sprang out of his seat and pumped his fist several times in the air. That was a clean, fast run and Dallas, for the moment, was sitting pretty in first place.

At the end of the women's barrel racing, Dallas ended in second place overall and won a nice chunk of change to add to her overall year earnings. Nick couldn't have felt prouder if he'd been the one out there racing at breakneck speeds around those barrels.

When he saw the cowgirl, she was flushed red in the face from the thrill of competing and winning.

"Don't think I'm being condescending when I say this, Dallas—but I'm proud of you." Nick had followed her, as was his habit, back to the temporary barn that had been erected for the rodeo.

Dallas had stopped rinsing Blue's body to let him play with the end of the hose and lap some water into his mouth. She looked over at him with happy eyes. "Heck no, I'm not offended! It's nice to hear that someone's proud of you. I'm proud of me!"

As she always did, Dallas made sure that Blue was clean and fed before she tended to her own needs. Nick took her hand in his and they walked together toward her trailer. They had been going back and forth about how the night would unfold. Nick wanted Dallas to grab her stuff—a change of clothing and some toiletries—and come to the hotel to get ready for dinner. Dallas was balking at the idea, but she was showing signs of being swayed.

"Just let me win this one, Dallas. You've won your race already, haven't you?" he asked her.

Dallas reappeared in the doorway of her trailer. She looked at him, studied his face, really, and he could see those stubborn wheels turning.

"Fine," the cowgirl relented. "We'll do it your way for a change."

Dallas knew she could get used to a swanky hotel like the Four Seasons without any difficulty at all. Of course, Nick had taken one of the best suites at the hotel with an amazing view of the downtown Houston skyline. She was well aware of his taste—he liked the best. And it was that great taste that actually made her feel good about being his date—he thought that *she* was the best. He wasn't just after her to get her into bed; he genuinely liked her. He valued her. He listened to her and supported her in a way she'd ever really known with one person in her life, and that was Clint. Never with someone she had dated. Nick was in a category all of his own.

"How's it going in there?" Nick knocked on the bathroom door. "We've got reservations in an hour."

"It's goin' great," Dallas called back from her immersed position in a giant spa tub. She had already washed her hair; she had also tackled the forest of hair on her legs and under her armpits—she had to use two disposable razors to get to smooth skin. Now she was totally submerged in a tub of clean, hot water, her second go-round; she had used the complimentary bath oil per Nick's instructions. The water was so hot and it felt so good on her tired, sore muscles that she wanted to soak until the water went cold and she was as wrinkled as a raisin.

"Hmm." Dallas sank even farther into the water until her face was the only part of her body not submerged. "This is the life."

She stayed in that sweet-smelling water until it started to feel too cold. It didn't take her long to get ready once she got started and she emerged from the steamy bathroom with clean clothes, a little makeup on her face and her hair formed into damp ringlets down her back.

"*That* was possibly the most amazing bath I have ever had in my whole entire life," Dallas told her host. "Thank you."

Nick was dressed in a classic suit holding a glass of champagne. "My pleasure."

Her companion handed her a glass of champagne. "I can't believe I turned you down the last three times you offered. Were the other tubs as amazing as this one?"

"They were." He smiled as he raised his glass to her. "I knew you were going to say that."

"Here's to you, Dallas Dalton." Nick looked at her with that admiring gleam in his Brand-blue eyes. "I love to watch you work."

Dallas touched her glass to his and then took a sip of the champagne. It was bitter, which wasn't really her taste, but it was the gesture that mattered to her. She walked over to the large window with a view out to the Houston downtown skyline.

"Everything looks better from up here," she noticed.

Nick came up behind her; he was wearing cologne tonight—it had a woody, smoky scent that she liked very much.

"Are you ready for dinner?"

Tonight, there was something different in his voice— a sensual edge that she hadn't heard him use before. Her body responded naturally to that unspoken desire in a tingling little shiver that danced across her skin.

"Are you cold?"

Nick actually saw her shoulders jerk a little as that shiver reached her shoulders.

"No." She put her glass down on a side table near the window. "It was just the champagne."

Nick had reserved a private dining room at the hotel's Italian restaurant, Quattro, located in the cellar, in celebration of her success in Texas. But Dallas could feel the difference in the way this night was unfolding. Nick was signaling to her, loud and clear, that he wanted to take their relationship to a more intimate place.

How long had it been since she had let herself go there? She had gone through a couple of shallow relationships with cowboys. But she'd never been able to open her heart with any of them. So, she decided to focus on being the best single she could be. And other than the occasional moments of loneliness and the natural ebb and flow of sexual frustration, she had lived a very successful life as a single. What would it be like to let someone into her life in *that* way?

"I know you prefer beer, but I'd like you to let me introduce you to some of my favorite wines tonight."

"I'm game."

Dallas was fascinated by the setting Nick had chosen specifically for them. The private dining room was intimate with deep purple walls and unusual cork floors; the table was surrounded by bottles, and then more bottles, of wine. She felt as if Nick was trying to sweep her off her feet—and if that was his intention, it was working.

"I hope you like Italian."

Dallas took the offered menu with a thank-you to their waiter. "Don't often get it, but I love it."

She looked at the menu; she had been expecting spaghetti and meatballs, manicotti, pizza. Nothing on this menu looked familiar to her, and the names of the dishes were in Italian.

"Is something wrong?" Nick must have noticed the confused wrinkling of her brow as she looked over the menu.

She leaned closer to him to whisper, "This isn't my kind of Italian."

"This is real Italian food," he explained. "Trust me, you're going to love it."

That dinner with Nick sealed her growing feelings for the man in a way perhaps nothing could have. He made sure, in everything he said, in everything he did, to make her feel comfortable. Nick never acted superior or made her feel "less than" because she was unfamiliar with the food on the menu. He walked her through the options, ordered a full-bodied sweet red wine and started them with an antipasto for two. That was just the beginning. Several glasses of wine into the meal, the waiter brought her *pollo Milanese*, a breaded chicken breast with baby roasted potatoes, and an arugula-tomato salad. The plate was so beautifully designed that it seemed a shame to ruin the aesthetics by eating the food.

"Try this." Nick held his fork out for her to taste his entrée. He had ordered the gulf wild snapper with asparagus and she had to admit that it had a strong but wonderful taste. Following his lead, she fed him a forkful of her entrée.

"I feel like I'm always saying thank-you to you," Dallas noted between bites. "Like I'm not pullin' my fair share in this deal."

"That's not true," Nick said in a tone that was meant to dispel that notion from her head. "You give me more than a meal and a bath in a spa tub."

"Oh, yeah? What?"

Nick hesitated as if he was being cornered into saying something that he wasn't quite ready to say. He put down his knife and his fork; he looked at her face, he met her eyes without any pretense and said, "Dallas, I've been trying for a while to figure out what it is about you that makes me hop on a plane and fly to Texas just to eat a meal with you. And, I think I've finally figured it out."

Nick paused, his eyes locked with hers. She couldn't have looked away in that moment if she wanted to.

"I don't know how you're going to take this. But I feel more alive when I'm with you than I do anywhere else."

* * *

They lingered over dinner and enjoyed the music and the candlelight that had been provided just for their pleasure. Dallas wanted to linger there, and she had never really been one for "lingering" around the dinner table. She liked to eat on the go more often than not. But this was a different kind of night with a different kind of man. This was the kind of man a woman could consider rethinking her future plans for.

That night, in the candlelight, sitting next to Nick Brand, Dallas did something that she hadn't ever done in her life—she started to think about how handsome Nick's children would be. And for a woman who had already decided long ago not to go that route in her life, thinking about Nick Brand's children was a shock to her system. And it made her realize that her feelings ran much deeper for this man than she had previously imagined. It was very possible that she had fallen in love with Nick Brand.

The waiter cleared their empty wineglasses from the table and made a final offer for dessert, which they both declined. Nick charged the dinner to his room, signed his name and then looked at her as if she were more interesting to him than any sugar-based dessert could ever be.

"Dallas." He reached for her hands. "Dallas. I want to take you back to my room."

Nick held her gaze—she knew what he wanted from her. "Okay."

Her simple response didn't seem to satisfy him. So he added, "I can take you back to the arena if that's what you want."

"No." Dallas squeezed his hand. "That's not what I want."

* * *

Nick had thought about making love to Dallas often—but it wasn't the only thing that he thought about her. Making love to her would be an extension of the passion he felt for her in his mind and his heart. It had never been just about sex with her; he hadn't really been "just about sex" with any women in his most recent years. He wanted the physical to mean something more than gratification alone. That, he had thankfully learned in his escapades abroad, was hollow gratification at best.

In the light cast off from the Houston skyscrapers, Nick took Dallas into his arms and kissed her lips. Alone, with this woman, was what he had craved. He wanted to hold her, kiss her, feel her body against his— how far she would be willing to go tonight wasn't the point. He didn't have to rush to the climax so quickly like a college kid. No—he wanted to lie with her and hold her in his arms. He wanted to fall asleep with her; he wanted Dallas to still be there when he awakened.

"Dallas," he murmured as he dropped butterfly kisses on her neck. "Stay with me tonight."

Her body stiffened, but she didn't pull away from him. She wrapped her arms around his body and rested her head on his chest. Something had happened to this woman—Clint had alluded to it—and it was a barrier he was going to have to navigate, slowly, carefully, respectfully.

"I don't think I'm ready to make love."

Ever honest and blunt, that was the Dallas he had grown to love.

Love.

Nick guided her face upward so she could see his

face, read the truth in his eyes, when he said, "I just want to hold you, Dallas. Let me hold you."

Dallas was tired of letting her past dictate her future. It was time to lock the past away and embrace her future. She borrowed one of his plain white undershirts and rinsed out her mouth with the hotel's complimentary mouthwash. Nick was waiting for her in the bedroom; good as his word, he was wearing his boxers. He stood on one side of the bed and she stood on the other. The several glasses of sweet red wine had relaxed her body; the large bed, with its high pile of fluffy pillows, seemed like the most comfortable bed in the greater Houston area.

Nick took the first step and climbed into bed. He turned on his side, held the covers up for her and waited for her to join him.

She was standing at the crossroads of her own life— the safe road was not the road that led into Nick Brand's arms. It was time for her to take a chance; it was time for her to consider a life that didn't require her to be alone.

"Come to bed." Nick beckoned to her.

Dallas climbed into the inviting bed; the feel of the soft mattress and the soft sheets seemed so decadent after years of sleeping in bunkhouses or in her converted trailer. What Nick was offering her was comfort beyond anything she had ever experienced in her life.

Nick pulled the covers over their bodies. "Are you comfortable?"

"Yes."

Dallas squeezed her eyes shut and tried to focus on every wonderful sensation she was feeling. Nick curled his warm, masculine body around her, his arms holding her securely.

Nick was nuzzling his nose into her hair. She heard him sigh as his body curved around hers in the most comforting way.

"Nick?"

"Hm?"

How long had it been since she had been able to get these next words out of her mouth?

"I want to tell you somethin' about me," Dallas said quietly.

Nick lifted his head off the pillow. "What's that, baby?"

Dallas pulled Nick's hand closer to her body.

"When I was…" she started, paused and then started again. "When I was sixteen, I was—raped."

The word that had always stuck in her throat—the word that made it hard for her to connect with men—came out.

Nick was so quiet that she thought for a moment that he had fallen asleep without hearing her confession. But then he tightened his hold on her, pulling her into his body as if to show her that he would protect her.

"I'm so sorry, Dallas." Nick had a catch in his voice. "I'm so sorry."

"Just—" she burrowed her head into the pillow "—be patient with me."

Nick tightened his arms even tighter around her body. "Baby, we've got all the time in the world."

Chapter Nine

Dallas woke up the next morning wondering if she had imagined Nick telling her that he loved her. She had been a little pickled with red wine and exhausted from her last race in Texas. The bed, a little slice of heaven, had enveloped her in a cloud of fluffy, fresh-smelling pillows, a plush mattress without springs and a heavy comforter that made her feel cocooned. And the best part, of course, was being held by Nick. As with everything in life, she was, and always had been, an independent sleeper—she liked her space. She had never been much on spooning and snuggling. But perhaps she was going to have to change her position on the whole spooning issue, because she had spooned like a champ last night.

"Coffee?" Nick held out a cup of black coffee for her. She had a feeling that he had already added the one sugar; the man truly did have a romantic streak and he seemed to remember every little detail about her. It was surprisingly charming and masculine. As if she were finally experiencing how a real man treated a woman.

Her eyes were open, but she was still completely engulfed in pillows and blankets. Nick smiled down at her.

"You talk in your sleep." He reached out and brushed a rogue curl out of her eyes.

"Anything interesting?"

Nick sat down in a nearby chair. His normally on-point hair was mussed in a sexy way, there was a hint of morning stubble on his face and his shirt was unbuttoned, showing off a healthy patch of chest hair.

"If you're Blue." Nick smiled before he took a sip of his coffee. "I was hoping to at least rate a mention."

Dallas pushed herself upright and shoved her wild curls back off her face. She knew that she had to look like a damn mess right now, but Nick had been with her at Lightning Rock when she was smelling and covered in dust and dirt and mud. Any point in her life, save death, would probably be a better look for her as compared to then.

"It's not Lightning Rock coffee," Nick warned her.

"Thank goodness for small favors." She took her first happy sip, knowing that the caffeine would clear the cobwebs quick enough.

She couldn't remember the last time she'd slept late. After she decided to stay the night with Nick, she called a friend at the rodeo and arranged for them to make sure Blue got his breakfast. Nick called the airline and changed his boarding pass for a later flight. Now they had the whole morning to while away together.

"That is a beautiful view." She had no idea that she was such a high-rise-view kind of gal. But the Houston skyline drew her eye and held it—and it was just as beautiful to her whether it was day or night.

"You're a beautiful view," Nick said easily.

Dallas brushed off his compliment with a scrunched-up face and changed the subject. "My stomach feels like it's flopped upside down and inside out."

"Room service or restaurant? Your choice."

"Room service."

She sat across from Nick and put away a man-size breakfast of two eggs, scrambled, bacon, a biscuit, a side of French toast and toast with jam.

Dallas stood up and lifted her borrowed T-shirt a little, showing her belly. "Look at this. Can you believe I stuffed all that food in there?"

Nick was smiling, as he often did, at her. Then his smile faded and his eyes homed in on something she often forgot about nowadays.

Dallas squinted and looked out at the skyline. She shook her head a little to keep unwanted memories from floating into her mind.

"What's on your mind?" he asked when he noticed her shaking her head.

Sometimes her mind cycled back to the assault without her permission. At the sound of Nick's voice, she forced those broken thoughts back into the darkness and gave Nick a small smile. "Absolutely nothin'. Now."

While Dallas was in the shower, Nick cleared his emails so he could focus on his lovely companion. After he answered his final email, he closed his laptop and his thoughts naturally turned to Dallas. He couldn't say that he was surprised when Dallas told him that she had been assaulted when she was a teenager—all of those puzzle pieces had been put in place to make a clear picture of the cowgirl. His heart ached for her.

And, he knew now that he needed to tread very lightly with Dallas.

Nick got out of bed because he felt ridiculous waiting for the cowgirl as if he were expecting to make love. He wanted to make love to her—his body wanted her—but the last thing he wanted was to make her feel pressured.

But, to his surprise, Dallas wasn't dressed when she came out of the bathroom. Her hair was twisted into a turban on top of her head, and her body was wrapped in the hotel-provided robe. She smiled at him shyly and got back into bed. He loved the way her face looked freshly scrubbed—it was pink and dewy and pretty to his eyes.

"It's all yours. I saved a towel for you."

Nick showered, shaved and brushed his teeth. He followed her lead and pulled on a fresh pair of boxers but didn't get dressed. Before he left the bathroom, he hesitated over his travel case before grabbing a condom and taking it with him. If, by chance, Dallas was willing to make love, he didn't want to ruin the mood by having to go find protection.

He quickly dropped the condom in the drawer next to the bed and joined her under the covers.

"I just needed a little while longer," she admitted to him.

"I wish we could stay for another night," Nick said. This was the longest he snuck away from his life since he had been surprising her in Texas. It still felt too short.

"Hmm," she agreed, turning on her side toward him.

Tonight, he would be back in Chicago getting ready for another week of work, and Dallas would be hauling Blue back to Montana. They would be far away from each other, heading in opposite directions, once again.

This time, Nick didn't know how long it would be before he had a chance to see his Montana wildflower again.

The thought of not seeing Dallas for a while made Nick want to get closer to her now. He reached for her hand, threaded their fingers together.

"Have you told anyone about us?" he asked her.

"Don't really have anyone to tell."

"Clint."

"Yeah—but he's married to your sister."

He'd had a feeling that Dallas had kept this from her best bud because if his sister knew that he was traveling to Texas to pursue the barrel racer, Taylor would have been blowing up his phone.

Dallas pulled the towel off her hair and he caught the honey-and-lemon scent of the hotel's signature shampoo. The cowgirl surprised him by turning her body toward him, scooting closer and putting her head on his bare chest.

He craved this closeness with her; he wrapped his arms around her and kissed the top of her sweet-smelling head. Could she feel his heart starting to beat harder for her? Every part of his body, including his groin, was responding to the woman in his arms. He had gone to sleep with a hard-on, he'd awakened with a hard-on—he was so hard now it felt like his skin was going to split apart.

Dallas tilted her face up, and his lips naturally found hers. Their kisses began innocent and light, but he needed to deepen those kisses. He threaded his fingers through her damp hair, holding her head in his hand as he slipped his tongue inside her mouth. Kissing Dallas was like coming home—her lips were so soft, she tasted so clean and minty. He lost himself in those kisses.

His hand moved down to her hip; he squeezed her

hip in his fingers and pulled her body closer into his. This was the moment he had been wishing for—the moment when Dallas relaxed into his arms and let him get close enough to love her the way he had been wanting.

Nick kissed the side of her neck, then her collarbone. Dallas had her hand on his chest, her nails lightly scraping through his chest hair. The robe she was wearing slipped open and he caught a glimpse of her small breast with a hardened, rosy nipple. Dallas didn't recoil from the light touch of his fingertips on her breast; she pressed her breast into the palm of his hand, which he took as an invitation to keep right on loving her.

"Yes?" Nick met Dallas's eyes as his hand moved to untie the robe's sash.

Dallas gave a slight nod before she kissed him.

They explored each other with their hands and their lips, keeping their bodies close together beneath the covers. Nick had a sheen of sweat on his chest and on his legs, but Dallas had started to shiver in his arms, so he kept the blanket pulled up over their bodies.

"Are you okay?" he asked the woman in his arms.

"Shhh." Dallas put her fingertips on his lips.

Nick kissed her fingertips as his hand moved down to her muscular thigh. He'd never been in bed with a woman who was built like Dallas—her butt, her thighs and her arms were packed with muscle from her sport. He wanted to know what it was like to have those arms wrapped around him—he wanted to know what it was like to bury himself between those strong, beautiful thighs.

Dallas made the tiniest gasp when he slipped his hand between her thighs. She was wet with desire; if he had doubted her response to him because she had been so quiet, that doubt fell away the moment he felt how hot and slick she was between her legs. He was so focused on the feel of her that Dallas caught him by surprise when she snuck her hand through the front flap of his boxers.

Nick groaned with pleasure when she wrapped her fingers around his erection and squeezed tightly. He couldn't stop himself from moving back and forth in her hand; it felt so good to have her touch him.

"Hold on." Nick stopped moving when he felt his body wanting to climax. "Hold on."

He closed his eyes and held his body still until he pushed the feeling aside. Nick kissed Dallas deeply, before he said of the robe between them, "Get rid of this."

Dallas did his bidding and shrugged out of the robe. Her eyes were on him when he stood up, stripped his boxers off and pulled the drawer open to get the condom he had placed there.

Nick let Dallas watch him unwrap the condom and then roll it onto him. He wanted her to see him—to see what was about to be inside her.

Skin to naked skin, Nick covered Dallas's body with his, settling himself between her thighs, teasing her slick opening with his tip.

"You're shaking." Nick rested his forehead on hers. "Baby—you're shaking."

Dallas wrapped her arms around his back, opened her thighs wider for him and lifted her hips to take him inside of her.

"Just hold me tighter."

Nick joined their bodies together and held her tightly as they found a natural rhythm that brought them both pleasure. He had never made love like this—so close, so quiet, so intimate. He kissed his cowgirl, taking her breath into him, tasting her, wanting to go deeper, wanting to last longer. More than anything he had ever known, loving this woman was a feeling he had craved but never found. Until now. Until Dallas.

"Are you coming?" Nick felt Dallas's body tighten and shudder.

He raised his head—he wanted to see her face as she found her bliss in his arms. The look on her face as she climaxed was so beautiful, so sexy, he wanted to join her. As Dallas made another little whimper, Nick lifted his body upward, braced his arms and pressed himself deeper into her center. Then he began to thrust into her, fast, hard—one last thrust and he threw back his head and groaned.

Dallas watched Nick climax, admiring how handsome he was in that moment. She had felt his erection last night, and this morning. She knew how much he wanted to make love. Even when she had first awakened, she wasn't sure that she could let her guard down with Nick in that way. But after breakfast, while she was showering, her mind had started to imagine what it would be like to feel Nick inside her. Her mind wanted to make love, her heart wanted to make love and when her body came on board, she emerged from the bathroom with lovemaking in mind.

Nick opened his eyes, so blue and clear, and stared down at her.

"Are you okay?" he asked, his chest rising and falling from the exertion.

Dallas reached out her arms so he would come back to her. It felt so good to have his weight on her—to feel him inside her—it was difficult for her to imagine that she had deprived her body of this experience for such a long time.

They were damp with perspiration, hot and still feeling languid with pleasure from their lovemaking. Nick left her for a moment to dispose of the condom, but he returned to hold her again. From her vantage, it seemed that Nick didn't want to let her go. He had held her like he meant it when he told her last night that he loved her. And even though she couldn't bring herself to say the words back to him, no matter how many times she tried while they made love, she felt as if she had fallen for Nick. This must be what love felt like.

Nick rolled onto his back and rubbed his eyes. "I have to let you go."

Dallas had her hand over his heart and her head resting on his shoulder. "I have to let you."

Nick hopped in the shower and rinsed off their lovemaking, but Dallas wanted to keep Nick's scent on her body for a while longer. She pulled on her jeans and boots and kept his T-shirt as a keepsake. Nick came out of the bathroom fresh from the shower and carrying a hanger with a pair of pressed chinos.

"I take it I'm not getting that back?" he said.

Dallas gathered her crazy hair back into a ponytail at the nape of her neck. "Souvenir."

Nick pulled on his chinos, zipped up the zipper, but left the top button undone. He walked over to her and put his arms around her.

"People usually take souvenirs to remember things they'll never see again." He was studying her so seriously. "You aren't trying to tell me something, are you?"

The truth was, making love with Nick was a calculated risk—there was a chance that she'd just given herself to a man she'd never see again. But then again, wasn't everything in life tied to risk?

"No." She tugged her body out of his arms.

Nick tried to lighten the mood in the room, which had turned more somber now that they were preparing to go their separate ways.

"You aren't a love-'em-and-leave-'em cowgirl, are you?"

Dallas crossed her arms in front of her body. "You can come see me anytime you want."

Nick, who had to get to the airport, had returned to dressing. He shrugged into his button-down shirt. "I wish I could see you tomorrow."

It sounded sincere, and at this point she didn't have any reason to doubt him. Nick wasn't a troll—he didn't have to fly all the way to Dallas to get a date. She believed that this strong attraction she was feeling for him was entirely mutual between them.

"That's not possible." She turned away from him so she could admire that incredible high-rise view one last time.

"No." Nick tucked in his shirt and buckled his belt. "But that doesn't change the fact that I wish it were."

Nick packed up his overnight bag, and after one last look at the view, Dallas left the lovely Four Seasons room. They rode down together in the elevator in silence—the conversation that had flowed so easily between them had dried up.

The valet brought the Porsche around to the front of the hotel, and Nick held the passenger door open for her before he took his place behind the wheel.

"You spoiled me rotten to the core this weekend,"

Dallas said as Nick put the car in gear and headed back to the arena.

"That was my goal." Nick smiled at her.

Dallas leaned back in the bucket seat and watched the Houston skyline pass by. In less than an hour, she planned on loading Blue into the trailer and getting on the road back to Montana. She'd drive as long as she could stay awake and then she'd pull over in a truck stop to sleep. No more heavenly Four Seasons bed for her; no more fabulous Four Seasons spa tub.

When they arrived at the arena, many of the exhibitors had already left—the parking lot was nearly empty.

"I'm worried about you getting such a late start." Nick had followed her to get Blue from the stables and bring him to her trailer.

"Don't be." Dallas waved her hand to brush away his concern. "Blue and I do this all the time."

Nick had his hands in his front pockets, standing out of the way so she had room to lead Blue in a small circle and then let the quarter horse walk into the trailer. Dallas shut the trailer gate and locked it.

"You'd better git." She wiped her hands off on her jeans. "They're gonna take off without you."

Nick took his hands out of his pockets and put them on either side of her face. He kissed her gently, sweetly, poignantly. "I'm going to miss being with you, Dallas."

For Dallas, goodbyes were uncomfortable. She'd rather just give a quick wave and be done.

"Text me when you land." She gave his chest a pat with her hand.

Nick let her go. He slipped on his sunglasses and backed away. "Text me when you pull over tonight."

Dallas watched Nick while he walked back to his

rental car—he gave her one last wave before he got in the Porsche and drove away.

Now that he was gone, the time they had spent together seemed like a dream. This was reality. She was back to being Dallas Dalton, roaming barrel racer.

Dallas put on her cowgirl hat and checked on Blue one last time to make sure he was secure, before she climbed into her cluttered mess of a Bronco, cranked the engine and set a course for Montana.

Chapter Ten

Hauling Blue from Texas to Montana was slow going and it took Dallas an extra day to get back to Bent Tree Ranch. This was the first time that she was returning from the road without the option of camping out at Lightning Rock or crashing with Clint. Normally, she wasn't opposed to bunking in the dorm with all the cowpokes—their burping and carousing didn't bother her—but somewhere along Interstate 90, Dallas started to feel sick. She was hot, then cold. She was sweating and then clammy and cold. She had to pull over several times because she was too nauseated to drive. It had to be that she picked up the stomach flu somewhere along the way, and by the time she, thankfully, pulled her trailer onto Bent Tree property, she was certain she was running a fever.

"You *are* running a fever." Barbara Brand took the thermometer out of her mouth and read it. "My goodness, Dallas—you need to take some medicine and get straight into bed."

Dallas had been feeling too lousy to go to the bunkhouse, so she'd ended up going to the one place she knew she could get some help: Barbara Brand's kitchen. "Now that Pop's gone and Clint's married—I'm not sure where I've got to go."

Barbara stared at her for a couple of blinks with blue eyes that reminded her of Nick. "You'll stay here."

Dallas couldn't remember a time when someone cared for her when she was sick the way Barbara did. Nick's aunt loaded her up with over-the-counter medicines to help bring down the fever and quiet her roiling stomach. She cooked up some chicken noodle soup with bland crackers and then drew her a hot bath, bundled her up in warm clothes and put her to bed so she could break her fever. Hank came in during the process, kissed his wife on the cheek and wished her well, before he headed to his office. Hank was used to his wife taking in strays—that was just part of the bargain he got when he married Barbara.

For a week, Dallas was stuck in bed, fighting a fever, aches and chills. A day into her stay at the main house at Bent Tree, Barbara had Hank bundle her up in a blanket and take her to town to see the doctor. She was diagnosed with the flu, given Theraflu and some steroids to quicken her recovery. Hank brought her back to the ranch and Barbara tucked her back into bed. She was too sick at the time to really think about it, but it did strike her as strange later that she was a woman full grown, in her thirties, before she had ever experienced someone tucking her into bed.

"Good morning!" Barbara breezed into the guest room where she had been staying. "How are you feeling today?"

Dallas squinted when the curtains were drawn to

let the daylight into the room. "I think my fever finally broke last night."

Barbara came over to the bed and felt her forehead with the back of her hand. "You're cooler. That's good news."

"I'm glad to see he's been keeping you company," Nick's aunt said of the large black cat curled up at her feet.

"He's barely left my side all week."

Barbara stopped to scratch the feline on the chops. "You're such a good boy, Ranger."

Dallas sat upright in bed. She needed to get up today—her body felt stiff and cramped from being stuck in bed all week.

"Do you feel up to coming down for breakfast?" Barbara paused in the doorway.

Dallas nodded. "I'll be right down."

Nick's aunt had cleaned her clothing and left them in a folded pile on a nearby chair. Dallas got herself dressed before she headed down to the kitchen. Following closely behind her was the Brand family feline, Ranger, who had purred for her and kept her company for days. Perhaps he saw that she was better now too.

"Let's see if you can hold this down today." Barbara had already made her a soft-boiled egg with a plain piece of unbuttered toast.

Dallas hated soft-boiled eggs—they were, in her opinion, inedible under any circumstances. But she was a guest at Bent Tree; she'd suffer through eating it.

She took a bite, chewed the egg quickly and rinsed it down with water as fast as she could.

"Coffee smells too good." Dallas looked longingly at the coffeepot on the counter.

"I could give you a tad—see how it goes."

Her first sip of coffee in a week tasted so good. It canceled the taste of that horrible soft-boiled egg. With the coffee, she managed to get through the breakfast Barbara had made for her.

"I'm glad to see you feeling better." Barb cleared away her plate.

Now that she *was* recovering, it amazed her how quickly she went downhill and how kind Barbara was to take her in. "I don't have a way to thank you."

Barbara joined her at the table. "You're Davy's daughter. You're family."

She'd never really thought of the Brands as family, but she knew that Hank had promised her father that he'd watch out for her. Dallas was used to taking care of herself, so that promise was between friends and didn't have anything to do with her. Until now.

"I'm gonna have to start thinkin' about gettin' a place to pitch my tent." Dallas voiced her concern aloud. It hadn't hit her before, but it did now—without Lightning Rock as a home base, she was technically homeless now.

"I was thinking about that," Barbara agreed. "What about the tree house?"

Of all the options that had been cycling through her mind, the tree house on Bent Tree property hadn't been in the equation. Hank had a tree house built for Barbara for one of the wedding anniversaries. It wasn't a typical tree house—it was a small gingerbread house in the trees, complete with a small kitchen, a bathroom, a living room and a spiral staircase leading up to a loft bedroom. There was a small barn nearby because Barbara liked to ride her horse to get to the tree house.

"I have money." Dallas frowned. She wasn't a charity

case. She'd just never thought of settling anywhere—
up until now, she hadn't been forced to think about it.

"Then pay us rent," Barbara countered. "I always
hate to think of it empty, going to waste. Hank and I
don't get out there anymore. It's perfect for you and
Blue. When you feel up to it, go take a look at it. If you
want it, we'll talk money."

Dallas had a moment to consider the offer because
the landline rang. Barbara answered the phone and
when she heard Nick's name, Dallas knew that he was
calling his aunt looking for her. She hadn't returned any
of his texts since she got sick—she didn't feel like talking to anyone. It wasn't a deliberate attempt to worry
him; she wasn't used to being accountable to anyone
but herself.

"She's right here," Dallas heard Barbara say. "Do
you want to talk to her?"

Barbara stepped out of the kitchen after she handed
the phone to her. Dallas was sure that Nick's aunt had
an inkling, after this phone call, that their relationship
might have progressed beyond friendship.

"Hello?"

"Dallas." Nick's voice sounded tense with worry.
"Thank God you're okay."

Nick hung up, feeling an uncomfortable mixture of
anger and relief. The last time he talked to Dallas, she
was leaving Wyoming and crossing into Montana. She
had mentioned on their last phone call that she wasn't
feeling right—she was tired and had a headache. And
then she fell off the radar. Who did that? Who just
stopped communicating?

Dallas Dalton.

"Nick! What are you doing down here? I thought we were going to catch up?"

Brit Darling-Hammond, a longtime friend and occasional lover when they were both between relationships, came down to the bottom deck of his parents' yacht. Ever since he was pursuing a relationship with Dallas, and at the same time starting a new job, he'd neglected his gang of weekend warriors. The weekend after his trip to Houston, he tried to make up for lost time and organized a yacht party on Lake Michigan for his friends.

"Business call." Nick put his phone in the pocket of his shorts.

Brit sat down on the couch next to him. She was exactly the type of woman he'd imagined would be his wife down the road—her family were members of the same country club, Brit had graduated summa cum laude from Stanford Law, and she was flat-out undeniably beautiful. Any features that hadn't been perfect at birth had been shaped through plastic surgery—she didn't have a wrinkle on her lovely face, her makeup was always flawless and she appreciated good clothing. Yet they had never really gotten their relationship up and running. They were friends, they had a good time in bed, but that had been as far as he could go with Brit.

Brit had her hand on his arm; she leaned close enough that her full breast brushed against his body. She'd been between relationships for a while and had started giving off "friends with benefits" signals.

"You planned this party for all of us and we have hardly seen you," she complained.

"I know," Nick apologized—he had been distracted by Dallas going radio silent. "I'm sorry."

Brit leaned close enough to nip at his earlobe—they

had been together enough that Brit knew exactly how to get him turned on quickly. Nick's body responded—Brit smelled like suntan lotion, she was wearing a bikini that would be very easy to remove and he had always enjoyed taking Brit to bed. But the harder he got, the more irritated he became. Nick stood up to break the sexual tension between Brit and himself.

"I met someone," Nick told his friend. That would make her back off—that was their deal. They didn't interfere with each other's chances to find that "love connection" that they didn't have with each other, even though, on paper, they should have been a perfect fit.

Disappointed, Brit said, "I hadn't heard."

He was losing his erection and he was glad for it. "It's new."

Brit stood up, adjusted her bikini top, her gold bangle bracelets tinkling with every movement of her tanned arm. "She can't be from here. I would have heard."

"Do you want to go back topside? Get a drink?"

"Oh!" Brit rebounded quickly from the idea of a sexual tryst. She linked her arm with his as they walked up the stairs to the top deck. "So it's a secret. You know how I am with a secret."

Brit was the group's Sherlock Holmes. Now that she knew he was holding back his cards, she would be relentless in her search to out him. He hadn't been able to figure out his feelings for Dallas—he hadn't been able to figure out how they were going to fit into each other's lives, and then when Dallas disappeared on him, it scared him. The fear of losing her outweighed his worry about how things were going to work out between them. He loved her; he wanted to be with her. The question he needed answered now: did the cowgirl want to be with him?

It took a solid four weeks, but Dallas had fully recovered from the flu and had settled in nicely in the tree house. It was her own space—something she hadn't ever really had. She had loved her nomadic life, but this was a nice way to experience life too. Stability. What a novel concept. So novel, in fact, that she had decided to take a longer break from barrel racing. She had enough money saved up from her winnings in Texas; the rent on her tree house was reasonable. Blue deserved a break and so did she.

A knock on the tree house door sent Dallas running down the spiral staircase. "Coming!"

Dallas swung open the front door; Nick was standing in her doorway.

"You found me." She stepped back so he could come into her home.

"Took me a minute," Nick admitted. "I'd forgotten about this place."

Nick took his duffel bag off his shoulder and set it on the floor. Dallas shut the door behind him, touched Nick's arm and hoped that he would take her into his arms. She knew that he was still upset with her—he had a legitimate beef—but she had missed him. She had missed him more than she could express in words.

Nick turned toward her wordlessly and pulled her into his arms. They stood for several minutes, hugging each other, glad to be back together. Nick kissed the top of her head, as he liked to do, and then he tipped her chin up so he could kiss her on the lips.

Dallas took his hand and led him to the two-seater

couch in the cozy living room. They sat down on the couch, their legs pressed closely together, their hands clasped.

"Please don't ever fall off the radar again, Dallas." Nick slipped his hand beneath her hair.

"I promise, Nick. Never again. I didn't mean to make you worry—I've never had someone out there worrying about my every move. Next time, you'll be the first one I tell."

"You're important to me, Dallas. You matter to me." Nick held on to her hand. "It took time for this connection I have with you—these feelings that I have for you—to work itself out in my mind."

Dallas dropped her forehead onto his shoulder with a laugh. "We are an odd pair."

"Does that matter?"

"Not to me. You?"

"No." Nick's eyes roamed her face. "Dallas. I love you."

He had never said that to her before; she had felt his love, in the way he treated her—in the way he held her and made love to her. But to hear the words—it felt like a dream.

Dallas stared into Nick's bright, clear blue eyes and wanted to be able to say that she loved him too. Her heart knew that it was true, but she couldn't get her mouth to form those words. Instead, she decided to fill the void of her absent words with a kiss.

It wasn't long before their reunion led them to the loft bedroom upstairs. Dallas's body had been reawakened in Houston and she had been wanting to make love with Nick in the worst way.

"You're so beautiful, baby." Nick tightened his arms around her body. "So beautiful."

Nick loved her slow and long; he took his time as if he was savoring the feeling of making love to her. He kissed her as he moved inside her, caring about her pleasure more than his own. She loved it when he was deep inside her, his groin pressed tightly against her own; she loved it when he kissed her neck and murmured sweetly in her ear that she was beautiful.

"Are you coming?"

She opened her eyes, knowing that he was watching her in her pleasure. In his eyes, she saw that he loved her. It was there for her to see.

"Yes." She gasped the word and closed her eyes as the orgasm fanned out across her body. So sweet. So sweet.

Soon after her orgasm began, Nick quickened his thrusts to join her. She let her thighs fall farther apart, trusting him to go deeper and harder. Knowing that he wouldn't hurt her.

Nick tensed above her, his arms braced on either side of her. Dallas opened her eyes to watch him climax. A thought flashed in her mind—this was what Nick would look like if he ever gave her a child.

Ever since he had met Dallas Dalton, his life plan had gone all wonky. First he was chasing her to Texas, and now he was in a tree house in Montana. So far, it wasn't interfering with his work—but it could if he didn't get things settled with her.

"I want you to come visit me in Chicago." Nick was propped up on a pile of pillows in Dallas's bed. He had the cowgirl exactly where he wanted her: in his arms.

"When?"

"Why not now?" He wanted to pull that Band-Aid off as soon as possible. She needed to meet his mother— God help them all—and she needed to see him in his natural element. In the city, where he felt at home.

"You want me to go back to Chicago with you?"

"That's what I want."

Dallas dragged her short fingernails through his chest hair, which seemed to be a favorite activity when they were together in bed. "I have a couple of weeks left before I have to start training hard and getting back on the road." She paused in thought again, then added, "I can go to Chicago for about a week, if it'll make you happy."

He wasn't sure it was going to make him happy— but they both needed to see if there was a way for them to blend their lives. That was where this was going, or else what were they doing?

After they had agreed that Dallas would fly back to Chicago with him, they went downstairs to raid the refrigerator. Dallas had stocked the kitchen in anticipation of his visit, and the cowgirl actually cooked for him. It wasn't fancy, but it was edible—chicken, vegetables and mashed potatoes.

At dusk, they went out to tend to Blue together and then they went for a walk, holding hands as the sun disappeared behind the mountains in the distance. Just as night had fallen and darkness enveloped the surrounding landscape, Dallas and Nick climbed the wraparound stairs leading up to the front door of the tree house.

"Are you tired? Or do you want to stay up for a while?" his cowgirl asked him.

"I want to go to bed."

Nick wasn't tired—he wanted to make love to Dallas again. Once upstairs, Nick undressed his woman, kissing her naked skin each time he removed a piece of clothing.

"I want you to ride me," Nick said.

The fantasy of Dallas riding him, his hands on her strong thighs, her head flung back, had become one of his favorite images he used to relieve his sexual tension; once he realized that he didn't want to be sexual with any woman other than Dallas, regular masturbation became an absolute necessity.

Now that it was dark in the room, perhaps Dallas would let the covers fall away from her body. He would love to look at her naked body while he loved her—her stocky, strong body was, as it turned out, the perfect fit for him.

Nick lay back on top of the covers; Dallas straddled his body and he helped her guide herself down his thick shaft until their bodies were as connected as they could be.

"My goddess." Nick ran his hands down her stomach to her thick thighs.

Unlike the other times they had made love, this time Dallas seemed to like being in charge. With her hands braced on his chest, Dallas rocked her hips like she was riding in a saddle, giving off soft, sexy moans. Nick waited until Dallas had her first orgasm before he swung his legs to the side, stood up with her in his arms.

"Hold on." Nick spun them around so when they fell back on the bed, he was on top of her. The maneuver didn't work as smoothly as he had imagined.

Dallas laughed, something she had never done when they made love. And this time she wasn't shaking in his arms. He knew, implicitly as he had known with so many things about this woman, that her trust in him had grown.

Nick held her face in his hands, kissed her lightly and said, "Did you say that you loved me?"

"Uh-uh."

"That's good." Nick pressed his body harder into hers. "Because I love you."

Dallas wrapped her strong legs around his hips and they moved together as if they had been lovers for years. Nick felt Dallas begin to orgasm for a second time and he cried out her name as he found his own release deep within the woman he loved.

Nick was the last of the two to go to sleep. It stunned him that he had actually considered what it would be like to make love to Dallas without a condom. He hadn't really considered children as an option in his life—having fun and building a career had been his priorities. With Dallas, he might just want something different. Not any time soon, but one day down the road, he'd like to see her pregnant with his child.

Chapter Eleven

Nick bought her first-class tickets to Chicago over her objections. Nick had shelled out a lot of money for their dates, and even though she prided herself on her independence, she believed that it was right for a man to pay for the date. But a plane ticket? No dice. She had money for coach—that was her budget—but Nick wanted her to sit with him on the trip back to his hometown and he ordered the ticket online, end of discussion.

Once on the connecting flight to Chicago, Dallas was actually glad that Nick had insisted on buying her a seat next to his. She'd traveled a lot in her life—most of her life was traveling—but the traveling she did had mostly involved driving. She had flown twice in her life. This plane was massive and jammed full of adults and kids and college students. Dallas didn't like it when something made her feel out of control—this plane made her uncomfortable.

"You almost done?" Dallas glanced over at Nick, who had been on his phone and laptop nonstop ever since the crew cleared the use of technology.

It took him a moment to look up from his phone. When he did, Nick's face had tension in it that she was accustomed to seeing.

"I'm sorry—this is for my work."

"All right." How many times had she told him that she couldn't talk on the phone or have dinner because of her work? A lot.

"I promise that I will carve out as much time as I can to show you Chicago," Nick said this while he typed out an email on his laptop.

"But…" He looked over at her. "You know that I have to work."

Dallas did know that he had to work. In theory. When she agreed, on a whim as was her nature, to go to Chicago, the visual of what the week would be like in the third-largest city in the country was only a fuzzy outline. Now, just seeing the change in Nick, from easygoing Nick to glued-to-his-electronic-devices Nick, her week in Chicago was starting to come into focus. She was going to be alone for much of the time. And even when Nick was with her in person, she had a feeling that the phone and the laptop were going to be his constant mistresses.

"Chicago, baby." Nick reached for her hand.

The Fasten Your Seat Belt message forced Nick to put away his phone and laptop; he was now looking out the window with her, and seemed excited for her to catch her first glimpse of a city that she knew he loved.

"I want you to love it," Nick added.

Dallas wanted to love Nick's city too. She really did. As the sprawling city came into view, Dallas thought, much like the Houston downtown skyline, that Chicago's downtown skyline was a beautiful scene to behold. Yet the miles and miles of roads and buildings and homes that fanned out away from the city center made her acutely aware of the fact that Nick's hometown was inhabited by *millions* of people.

Chicago O'Hare was crowded and hot and it took some jostling to get their luggage from the carousel. When she looked around at the wide spectrum of people in the airport, there were so many different races and manners of dress, but she didn't see many Stetsons.

Nick walked fast in Chicago; in Montana and Texas, he had been more relaxed. They picked up his Jaguar, and from the second Nick got behind the wheel and fought his way into bumper-to-bumper traffic to the time they pulled into valet parking at his downtown condo, he was so intense and frustrated. And yet he loved the city. All the way from the airport to his condo, Nick pointed out landmarks and places he spent his time. He seemed to thrive on the congestion and the frantic energy of the city.

Dallas looked out the passenger window to the signage on the building: the Ritz-Carlton.

Why were they at a hotel?

"I'm not stayin' with you?" she asked.

Nick handed his keys to the valet. "This *is* where I live."

A different valet opened her door and offered her a hand. Nick jogged around the front of the car; he thanked the valet, but he was the one to help her out onto the sidewalk.

"Welcome to my world." Nick offered her his arm.

"What about our bags?" Dallas looked behind at her small rolling bag.

"Don't worry. They'll get to us. Come on. I'm excited to show you the view."

Nick lived on the twenty-second floor of a forty-story building in downtown Chicago. The lower part of the building was the Ritz-Carlton Hotel.

"I'm renting the place from my parents," Nick explained as he put the key in the door. "I love living in this building—it's close to work, and I've been thinking about buying the condo."

Nick opened the door for her and let her walk inside the condo first. Immediately, she saw the view. He had told her that he had a surprise for her. He loved to surprise her—Nick knew how much she loved the downtown view in Houston. To have that kind of view for the week? This was a wonderful surprise.

"Nick—the *view*!" She smiled at him.

"I knew you'd love it."

"I do." Dallas walked through the narrow entrance way, through a curved arch that led out to an open-concept living and dining room. Dallas noticed the lovely, wide-plank dark wooden floors and the dove gray of the walls, but she was all about the wall of glass that led out to a small patio.

Nick anticipated that she would want to see the outdoor space first. Dallas walked out onto the small patio; she rested her hands on the railing and looked down. Nick came up behind her and wrapped his arms around her body.

"You're looking down at the famous Magnificent Mile," he told her. "And that tall skinny building right there—that's the Willis Tower, one of the tallest buildings in the Northern Hemisphere. I'm going to take you there tonight."

Dallas couldn't see herself living in a downtown

high-rise full-time, but the beauty of Nick's view was undeniable.

"What do you think?" He moved her hair out of his way so he could put his chin on her shoulder.

What did she think? She thought it was noisy with the sirens and horns blowing, and it was too crowded, and there was a lot of exhaust.

"I love your view." Dallas wanted to tell her man the positive truth about his hometown. She knew that he was anxious for her to love it as much as he did.

This answer seemed to make Nick happy—he turned her in his arms and kissed her in that sweet, gentle, easy way of his.

"I love you," he said in between kisses. "I love you."

Nick gave her a chance to soak in his giant tub before they went on their first Chicago adventure. According to his calendar, he had packed their schedule every night and for the upcoming weekend. Dallas was up for it. She had her doubts, but she wanted to be open to falling in love with Chicago. After all, she was open to falling in love with one of its best sons.

"Maybe leave the hat here," Nick suggested.

Honestly, even on the occasions she got dressed up for rodeo award ceremonies, she still wore a hat. Everyone did. It would feel strange not to wear it.

Dallas looked at Nick, as always, dressed crisply in chinos, a button-down and loafers, and his hair cut high and tight. She thought about the suggestion and ultimately decided "when in Chicago…"

"You look great." Nick smiled at her approvingly as he buttoned his sleeve cuff.

She thanked him and returned the compliment. Nick

shrugged into a sports coat, gathered his wallet and keys, and then held out his hand for her. "Let's go have some fun!"

Nick didn't get the valet to bring his car around; instead, he offered her his arm and they started to walk up Erie Street.

"What's there to do at the Willis Tower?" His excitement for having her in his city was infectious. It was hard not to smile.

"My cousin and her husband are having an event on the ninety-ninth floor."

"Which cousin?"

"Jordan."

Dallas stopped walking and gaped at Nick. "Are you tellin' me that your cousin Jordan is here? Right now?"

"That's right."

Dallas hit Nick affectionately on the arm. "I haven't seen her since we were kids!"

Barbara and Hank had five children, the two oldest boys twins, Luke and Daniel, a middle child, Tyler, and then the youngest twin girls—Jordan and Josephine. Jordan, she remembered, was a tomboy daredevil like her.

"What's their exhibition?" Dallas asked, more excited now to get to Willis Tower than she had been just a moment before.

"A collection of photographs," Nick explained. "Jordan's husband, Ian, was a really well-known fashion photographer—a couple years back he lost his eyesight and he had to quit. With Jordan's help, he's taking photographs again."

"The love of a good woman."

Nick squeezed her hand. "Exactly."

* * *

"Nicky!" Jordan Brand Sterling spotted them the minute they walked off the elevator.

Nick's cousin was a tall, willowy woman dressed in slim black pants and a figure-hugging top. Her hair was cropped short and colored a light lavender.

"Thank you so much for coming to support Ian." Jordan had this genuine openness about her smile that Dallas always liked. "Dallas! What are you doing here?"

Jordan hugged her cousin and then hugged her like they were long-lost friends. In a way, she supposed they were. "I'm visitin' with Nick."

A quick myriad of emotions passed over Jordan's pretty face: surprise, curiosity, acceptance. Jordan, who was nearly six feet tall in her bare feet, leaned toward her. "Thank God *you're* here. OMG! There's so much *stuffiness* in this thin Chicago air, a good dose of Montana will balance the mojo."

Jordan's excitement about her being in Chicago made her relax inside; she hadn't even realized how tense she had been holding herself.

"Come meet my husband," Jordan said. "Nick hasn't even met Ian! Weird, right? That's the good ol' Brand family dysfunction for ya."

Jordan introduced them to Ian Sterling, who happened to be one of the most beautifully handsome men she'd ever met in person. She didn't really believe that people like Ian existed in real life—he was tall with broad shoulders, chiseled jawline, very nice lips. And with Jordan on his arm, they were the beautiful couple in the room. Ian did wear special glasses with lenses that protected his eyes—a rare eye disease had taken his central vision, but he still had his peripheral vision intact. Sitting quietly beside Ian was a black service dog named Shadow.

After they talked for a few more minutes, Ian and Jordan went back to circulating the room to meet and greet their guests. Nick and Dallas stopped by the open bar, and Nick looked impressed, and a little surprised, when she ordered a glass of wine.

Together, they walked around the gallery of photographs—each photograph seemed to be more compelling than the next. Ian was still photographing women, but the women were a part of the scenery, not the main focus. Nature, color and the human body were all captured in such unique ways. Ian, even with his disability, or perhaps because of his disability, had focused in on details of life that most people would never notice.

Dallas loved it and thanked Nick for bringing her.

"I have one more thing I want to show you," he said with a secretive smile.

They said their goodbyes to Ian and Jordan; they parted with a promise that they would all get together again while the three of them were still in town.

"I'll come get you while he's working. We'll go find some trouble to get into," Jordan had told her.

"Where are you takin' me with that smile?" Dallas asked him as she stepped into the elevator.

Nick pressed the button to take them to the hundred and third floor. "You're going to love what's next."

Dallas stepped out of the elevator onto the hundred and third floor of one of the tallest buildings in North America and knew immediately why Nick had brought her.

"What a view." She took a deep breath. It was dusk and the lights of downtown Chicago were lighting up.

Nick took her hand and led her to where a small group of tourists were gathered. Beyond the tourists, the Skydeck Ledge, a clear floor that let you have a straight view one hundred and three stories down. Nick led the way, winding through the crowd until they were standing on the clear ledge.

Dallas loved adrenaline rushes, which was part of the thrill of barrel racing—standing on a clear floor looking straight down to the city street below made her heart start to race, and sent adrenaline shooting all over her body. She held Nick's hand, more out of excitement than any fear, and felt as if they were flying or falling.

After she had a moment to experience the clear ledge unfettered, Nick pulled her into his side and kissed her quickly so she wouldn't object to the public display.

"We'll come back again—during the day," Nick reassured her when they left the clear ledge. "On a clear day, you can see four states away."

For Nick, Dallas's first day in Chicago was a resounding success. She loved the condo view and the outdoor space, and *bonus*, his cousin from Montana, a childhood play buddy of Dallas's, was in town. Awesome luck on his part!

He brought his woman home, made love to her with the city lights streaming through the window and then went to his office to catch up on work while Dallas drifted off to sleep in his bed. He'd had women sleep over, of course—he'd been in relationships where the women had actually started to move some of their belongings into the closet—but having Dallas in his home, in his bed was a feeling he'd yet to experience. He felt whole—like everything was right in his world now that his wild-child Montana cowgirl was curled up beneath his covers.

Nick wanted the rest of Dallas's week to be as successful; he'd struggled with when to take Dallas home to meet the parents—should that be a beginning of the week or the end of the week kind of event. He had decided to get it over and done with. Everyone in the family knew that his mother was *difficult*. And he anticipated that she was going to become *very difficult* when she discovered that yet another one of her children had gone to the dark side and was dating "country folk." Honestly, he was surprised that he had fallen for someone like Dallas. Falling in love, he was discovering, wasn't a matter of choice—it was a matter of your heart finding what it wanted.

"Woo-*hoo*!" Jordan Brand hung over her cousin's balcony and let out a loud whoop. She spun around and leaned back against the railing. "Nice digs, eh?"

Dallas was happy to see Jordan. She had awakened late, barely remembering Nick giving her a kiss goodbye, ordered room service from the Ritz and then drunk several cups of coffee on the balcony. But as much as she loved the view, she was starting to feel stir-crazy just looking down at all the activity on the street below. Jordan's call to see if she wanted to hang out came at the exact right time.

Jordan fell into one of the balcony lounge chairs, one leg dangling over the armrest. She flipped her sunglasses onto the top of her head. "So—you and my cousin Nick. How'd that happen? I'm dying to know."

"Lightning Rock," Dallas said. "Nick helped me get Pop's affairs in order."

Jordan's playful expression changed to one of regret. "I was so sorry to hear about your father, Dallas. I have—really good memories of him."

"Thank you." Dallas tucked her foot underneath her thigh. "Sometimes I forget that he's gone. I half expect to find him right there at Lightning Rock."

"But—Nick helped you through it. Dad told me he was out there with you. He didn't mention anything about…" Jordan waved her finger back and forth "…the two of you…"

"We're still pretty new." Dallas noticed how similar Jordan's eyes were to Nick's. All these Brand kids had these incredible blue eyes.

Would she have children with those same blue eyes one day? The more time she spent with Nick, the more she started to think that she really would like to have a child. At least one—with Brand-blue eyes.

Jordan sent her an odd look. "Have you met my aunt yet?"

"No—not yet. I think we're havin' dinner with them one night this week."

"She's a pill."

"What do you mean?"

"I mean," Nick's cousin said, "she's a royal pain in the ass and everyone knows it, including Nick—so expect that she's going to be horrible. She runs around telling people that she is a direct descendant of President Washington—not true." Jordan rolled her eyes. "Don't listen to anything she says, that's all."

After they spent some more time catching up, Dallas told Jordan that Nick was taking her to the symphony and that she needed to get a dress for the evening.

"Well—shopping's really my sister and mother's area of expertise."

"I'm jeans and boots."

Jordan swung her leg off the armrest and stood up. "Let's go take a walk. There's a Bloomingdale's right up the road. Between the two of us, we'll be able to figure it out."

Dallas was genuinely thrilled with her outfit for the symphony. Jordan, who had more shopping skills than even she realized, helped her find a simple, sexy wrap dress, a pair of shoes with a low heel and a purse. When she looked in the mirror, it was hard for her to see herself in clothing so different than her typical uniform. It took some coaxing on Jordan's part to get her out of the dressing room; Nick's cousin had made her feel good about herself in that dress. The more she looked at her reflection in the mirror, the more she thought that Nick was going to love this look on her.

"I can't believe I bought a dress," Dallas said after they ordered lunch.

"You look like a boss in that dress."

"I've never owned a dress."

Jordan, who was drinking an extra-large Thai tea, put her drink down on the table with a thud. "Never?"

Dallas laughed a little. "Mom used to say that the only dress she ever got me to wear was my christening gown as a baby. I hated dresses. So after Mom and Pop split, and I chose to go with Pop—I never had anyone to fight with me 'bout wearin' a dress."

"Well—for what it's worth, you look really good in a dress."

"I'm excited to wear it now." Dallas tried to imagine the look on Nick's face when he first saw her in the dress. "I've done nothin' but try new things ever since I met Nick. That's partly why I like him so much."

Dallas looked off in thought and added, "I'm not so sure what I do for him, though."

Jordan took gulp after gulp of her drink until her straw was gurgling before she said, "That's obvious. You give my cousin someone awesome to love."

She was someone who didn't blush—but Jordan's words made her face and neck feel flushed, as if she *were* blushing.

"You know," Jordan said after a moment of thought, "if you want, we can get your hair and makeup done while he's at work tomorrow. Really freak Nicky out when he sees you."

"Yeah." Dallas reached up to touch her unruly mass of brown curls. "Let's do it."

Chapter Twelve

The night of the symphony, Nick was running late from the office. He hated that he had to spend so much time away from Dallas when she was in a strange city, but he couldn't take off so early on in his employment. Yes, his father had a lot of pull with the firm, but he wasn't his father. If anything, the partners at the firm expected *more* out of him because of his father. Sometimes he wondered if it was the best idea to follow in his father's exact footsteps; no matter how many times he asked that question, he couldn't imagine any other path than the one he was on. This was his path—his destiny.

"I'm sorry I'm late, babe!" Nick came in the front door of his condo.

He dropped his keys in a glass bowl along with his mail. "Dallas?"

"I'm almost ready!" Dallas's voice appeared to be coming from the master bedroom.

Normally, Nick would loosen his tie, get out of his suit coat and consider whether or not he would raid the fridge or order room service. Tonight, he didn't have time. He needed to make a quick pit stop and then hustle to the symphony. He had developed a love for the symphony when he was a kid; he hoped that Dallas would love it, as well. He appreciated that, even though Dallas hadn't been introduced to cultural events, she was open to the experience.

Nick passed up the fridge and headed to the master bedroom to find Dallas. He had missed her; knowing that his love was close made it difficult to concentrate on work. If he hadn't been booked with a working lunch, he would have come back to the condo. Nick checked his watch on his way down the hall; they had about five minutes to get out the door.

"Dallas?"

"Howdy, Mr. Brand."

Nick stopped in his tracks. The woman standing before him had his woman's voice, but that was where the resemblance ended. Dallas was wearing an above-the-knee, formfitting black dress with a crisscross halter neckline and a small, tasteful offset slit. Her hair—*her hair*—was straight and sleek and pinned back from her face. That face. He had always thought she was cute on the outside and beautiful on the inside. This woman—this version of Dallas—was a knockout with makeup on. He'd never seen her wear more than lip gloss and mascara.

Dallas pirouetted for him, showing off the back of the dress.

"What do you think?"

Nick shook his head in amazement at the cowgirl's transformation. She looked every bit a chic Chicago woman.

"Incredible." He walked to her. "You look incredible."

Nick leaned in to kiss her, but Dallas playfully dodged him. "Don't mess up my lipstick!"

"Your hair. It's…"

"I know," Dallas agreed. "You don't have to say it. It's tame, for once. But don't go gettin' used to it. It's temporary."

"Well." Nick reached out to touch the silky straight locks. "You should consider seeing if they can do this permanently. It suits you."

Dallas swatted his hand away from her hair. "Do you have any idea how long it took two women to get my hair like this? Lord help me, if it's even a touch humid out there, I'm gonna wind up looking like a cotton ball."

They caught a cab to the Chicago Symphony Center. Nick intertwined his fingers with Dallas's, noting how soft her hands were. Her nails were painted with a classy French manicure; the perfume she was wearing was new.

"I'm glad Jordan was in town to keep you company while I'm working."

"You and me both. She's been a godsend." Dallas rested her shoulder against his. "This was her doin', you realize."

"I figured. I owe her one."

He really did owe his cousin a debt of gratitude. The Chicago Symphony Center was the first place that Nick was taking his cowgirl where it was likely that they were going to run into friends of his parents. It was inevitable at a venue like this one. Now that Dallas was dressed to the nines, he wasn't as worried about the negative rumor mill reaching his mother's ears. She would have her say soon enough.

"Are you excited about the symphony?" He kissed

her hand instead of trying to kiss her on her perfectly outlined and painted lips.

"You have no idea."

Dallas wanted to know about his day—and she seemed genuinely interested in his profession. The rest of the taxi ride to the venue, Nick told her as much as he could about his work without divulging privileged client information. The fact that Dallas would sit and listen so intently to him, really listening, was a rare and beautiful trait to find in a partner.

"I'm worried I'm gonna fall flat on my face in these shoes," Dallas worried to him aloud. "I miss my boots."

"Hold on to my arm." Nick offered his arm. "You can lean on me."

Nick had secured seats in the Chicago Symphony Center for balcony seats. Their seats overlooked the symphony, which gave Dallas a wonderful bird's-eye view of the entire first floor. The room was grand, towering four stories high with curved ceilings and row after row of chairs covered in red velvet.

Nick's chair was facing the orchestra, set on a slight diagonal, so that his ear was close enough for her to lean in and whisper, "This is a dream."

The lights dimmed and the orchestra began to play Beethoven's Seventh. Dallas forgot about the shoes that were pinching her feet or the body-shaper undergarments that were making her feel like an overstuffed sausage beneath her dress; she forgot all about her discomfort and focused on the music. The horns and the strings and the piano—all the notes of the instruments swirled together into one unbelievable sound. Nick glanced back at her on several occasions, she assumed to make certain that she was having a good time—but she didn't take her focus off the orchestra. She leaned against the balcony railing and let the music envelop her. Dallas could feel the music in her body; it felt as if the music spoke to her soul in a way that nothing had before. Not even working with her horses.

"Do you want to get something to drink?" Nick asked her when intermission began and the lights in the gallery brightened.

"Wine?"

"Of course."

They moved with the crowd, slowly making their way out to the lobby. This was the part she hated about big cities—crowds. Even in a classy place like the Chicago Symphony Center, people were just too close for her comfort. She was so close to the person in front of her that she could read the tag on the back of her dress that needed to be tucked in—and she had someone so close behind her that she could feel their breath on her perfectly straightened hair.

Once out in the lobby, where she felt like she could breathe a little, she had to wait in a line for the ladies' room that had to be forty women deep. The symphony—yes; people at the symphony—no.

"I guessed a sweet red." Nick had a glass of wine ready for her.

"I need it after all that," Dallas complained. "I should've just hopped the men's line—I could'a shaved ten minutes off my time at least!"

"Nicholas! I thought that was you. Is your mom here tonight?"

Abigail Crane was the wife of a senior partner at the

firm and his mother's longtime golf partner. Of course, Abigail would be the person he would run into. Anything that Abigail detected as "not appropriate for our set" in Dallas would be immediately reported to his mother. He'd known it was a risk to put the symphony ahead of dinner.

"No. Mom didn't come tonight."

"Oh." Abigail glanced at Dallas with keen eyes. "That's too bad."

The socialite extended her hand to Dallas. "I don't believe we've met."

"Forgive my manners, Mrs. Crane. This is Dallas Dalton. Dallas, this is Mrs. Abigail Crane—she's married to one of the senior partners at my firm."

"Howdy." Dallas pumped Abigail's hand a couple of times.

Abigail reclaimed her heavily bejeweled fingers from Dallas; her lips pursed slightly before they smiled the slightest of smiles.

"Howdy?" Abigail had a raised eyebrow for him before she turned her attention to Dallas. "That's so quaint. Where are you from, dear?"

Nick stepped in and answered for Dallas. "She's from Montana—like my father."

The dress and the shoes, the hair and makeup, all made Dallas look the part, but the minute she opened her mouth, that high-country twang came out and ruined everything. He hadn't really noticed her country accent when they were in Texas and Montana—maybe it was because just about everyone else had a country accent too. But here in his city, her country twang stood out. And not in a way that he liked. God—he hated to admit it—but it embarrassed him.

Nick was grateful when their conversation was cut short; the lights flashed, signaling the end of intermission. Abigail waved her long, thin fingers weighted down by a collection of large solitaire diamonds.

"It was lovely meeting you," the socialite said to Dallas. To him, she said, "Be sure to tell your mom that I do hope she can make it to brunch at the club this Sunday. We have *so much* to talk about."

"I'll tell her." Nick smiled a warm smile that he didn't mean at all. He'd never liked Abigail, but she was the only woman catty enough to be friends with his mother. They were, and always had been, two peas in a very judgmental, snobbish pod.

"She seemed nice," Dallas said.

Nick stared at his companion—could she really be that naive about women?

"Except for that giant stick she had stuck up her hind parts."

As she usually did, Dallas made him laugh. Definitely not naive about women.

"Let's head back to our seats. Intermission is about over."

Dallas gulped down the rest of her wine and tossed the plastic cup into the trash. She took his arm so they could walk together back to their seats. The lights dimmed and once again the symphony began to play one of his favorite concertos. Now that Abigail had met Dallas, that pesky Band-Aid was ripped off—Abigail would be on the phone to his mother first thing in the morning, and his mother would have a preconceived notion of Dallas before he brought her home for dinner. Did he like the fact that there was a social hierarchy? Not really—not anymore. He used to thrive on elitism—but his time traveling to the Middle East and Europe had changed him. Yes, he was a part of the Chicago "upper crust"—he was also a man who had a heart. His heart wanted Dallas.

Throughout the second part of the evening, Nick tried to focus on the music and Dallas—she was fun to watch. Her face was priceless—so absorbed and enchanted with the music. But part of the time, he was thinking about what Abagail was going to say to his mother about Dallas. He already knew it would be negative—there was no doubt about that. Despite her obvious flaws, he loved his mother. It would have been nice to have his eventual marriage and children be a unifying force for his fractured family. That was not going to be the case if he married Dallas.

"You seemed to enjoy that." Nick put his arm around Dallas's back to guide her up the stairs and out to the lobby.

Dallas shook her head several times—when he got a chance to come up beside her and look at her face, he was completely surprised to see that her eyes were glassy with emotion.

It seemed to take Dallas a moment to find the words she wanted to say to respond. When they pulled away from the throng of people leaving the balcony seating, Dallas stopped and put her hand on his arm and looked up into his face. "That filled my soul."

Floored by her comment, Nick stared into Dallas's eyes. When he saw his favorite things through the cowgirl's eyes, he discovered new things to love, as well.

"You are lovely." Nick kissed her lightly on the lips—she had chewed most of her lipstick off her lips from biting them in excitement during the concert.

"Let's go home." Nick took her hand in his.

The minute he said those words, he knew what this trip was really about for him: finding a way to make a home with Dallas Dalton.

It had been a pleasure for him to undress Dallas after the symphony. She had kicked her shoes off with a vow never to wear them again, and he had unzipped the dress for her and kissed her bare shoulders as the dress slipped over her hips and onto the floor. He had picked her up, carried her to his bed and laid her down, with the downtown Chicago lights sending fingers of gold across her naked skin.

Dallas had watched him take off his suit jacket, her hair strewn across the bedspread. How pretty she had looked in that light. And how desirable. Tonight, he was going to try to love her in a new way—to kneel between her thighs and kiss her—taste her. He wanted to bring her to climax with his mouth. Perhaps tonight was the night that she would trust him enough to open herself up, physically and mentally—perhaps tonight she would trust him enough to be truly vulnerable.

After he stripped his clothes off, Nick had walked over to where Dallas was lying naked on the bed. Instead of getting on the bed with her, he did just as he had planned in his mind—he knelt down on the edge of the bed and ran his hands over her powerful thighs up to her curved belly.

"Come here." Dallas beckoned to him.

"No." Nick slid his hands beneath her legs to put her in the position he wanted. "You come here."

"Nick…"

"Dallas—if it doesn't feel right, I'll stop."

Nick moved her body so that her legs were dangling off the side of the bed. He gently pushed her legs apart. "Try to relax."

He massaged her legs, working his way to her inner thighs. He dropped a trail of small kisses from her knee all the way to that light pink flower between her legs. The moment he kissed her, the moment he put his mouth on her, Dallas grabbed the bedspread with her fists and her thighs clamped his shoulders.

He tasted her—so sweet, so delectable. Dallas made the tiniest whimper; this was the encouragement he needed to make love to her with his mouth and his tongue until he couldn't stand to not join his body with hers.

"Damn it!" Nick riffled through his bedside table drawer until he found a condom.

Dallas had one hand between her legs and the other on her breast. She was breathing heavily; he could see in her face that she needed the same relief he was after.

"Give me your hand." Nick held out his hand after he secured the condom.

Dallas put her hand in his and Nick had her stand up while he sat down on the edge of the bed.

"Wrap your legs around me," he ordered gruffly. All he could think about was sinking into her tight, wet warmth.

Dallas climbed onto his lap, sank down and took all of him in; skin to skin, flesh to flesh, their bodies felt like one body.

The woman in his arms held on to him so tightly he could feel how much she needed him. They kissed, their tongues joined, rocking together, pleasuring each other as they pleasured themselves.

"Hold me tighter," Dallas whispered into his neck.

Nick tightened his arms around her shoulders. He had loved her enough to know that she was building to a climax—and he wanted to get her there.

"Deeper," the cowgirl demanded. "Deeper, please."

Nick wrapped his arms behind her back, latched his hands over her shoulders and drove upward. He was so deep, so deep...

"Oh," he heard Dallas say on a breath. "God."

His cowgirl, who liked to whoop loudly in the show ring, was such a quiet lover. One day, he hoped he could get her to scream with pleasure.

"Come with me." Dallas kissed his neck, his jaw-line, his lips.

Her words triggered his orgasm and he shuddered in his lover's arms.

Nick held her body to him, keeping her on his lap. His head was resting on her chest, right above her beating heart.

"You're incredible." Nick leaned down and kissed her puckered nipple.

After they rinsed off in the shower, they came back to bed. They were satiated from a satisfying lovemaking session, and still in high spirits from the symphony. The light from the downtown buildings streamed into the large windows of his bedroom—he rarely shut the curtains because he loved the downtown lights.

Dallas lay in his arms, her back to him, her naked skin so warm and silky next to his hairy chest and legs.

"Dallas?"

"Hmm?"

"Do you think you could ever live in Chicago?"

The cowgirl didn't answer right away. She was so

still and so quiet that he started to think that she had dozed off and hadn't heard his question. But then she turned slightly in his arms, enough so she could look at him over her shoulder.

"No," she said in a soft voice. "I don't think so."

Nick had been rubbing his hand from her shoulder to her elbow, but his hand stopped moving when she answered him.

"What if there were a place outside the city where you could keep Blue?"

"I don't really know—I haven't thought about it, really."

Nick sat up a little. "You haven't thought about it at all?"

"Moving to Chicago? No."

Nick moved back so he could see her face. "I live in Chicago."

Dallas waited for him to continue.

"My goal is to follow in my father's footsteps and become a judge here."

"I think that's a real nice goal to have."

Nick didn't want to spend time talking in a circle— and perhaps this wasn't the best time to broach the subject. But if not now, when?

"Do you see a future with me, Dallas?"

Dallas pulled away a little too, tugging the sheet over her breasts. "I don't spend a lot of time looking into the future unless it has to do with barrel racing."

"I think it's time for us to start thinking how we can blend our lives. Yours and mine."

Dallas seemed genuinely surprised by his move toward a commitment. "I suppose I thought we were just feelin' things out."

Nick had always been someone who could zero in on what he wanted without much time for pondering. He knew that Dallas was the one for him.

"Oh, I felt you, baby." Nick pulled her back into his arms. "And now I've got to figure out how to keep you."

Chapter Thirteen

"Don't be nervous," Nick said to her as they approached his parents' Lincoln Park mansion.

Dallas wondered if he was trying to calm her down or himself—she didn't feel nervous. She'd never had an occasion to "meet the parents"; the men she had dated before were nomadic cowboys whose families were often states away. She was raised by Davy to believe that "either folks like you or they don't" and that was the end of it. She knew that she had self-esteem issues like most people, but Davy had drilled into her that no matter what people thought about her, it would only change who she was if she let it. Maybe she didn't know much, but she knew that.

"I'm doin' fine," she said.

They had experienced their first "lovers' disagreement" and she was trying to chalk it up to Nick being stressed about bringing her to his parents' house for dinner. She had wanted to wear her jeans and boots—they were clean and dressier than her work jeans and boots, but she felt like herself in them. It was fun to surprise

Nick with the dress, the makeup and the heels that hurt her feet. For her, it had felt like a Halloween costume. It wasn't her at all.

Nick, on the other hand, wanted her to wear the outfit she had picked out with Jordan for the occasion. He explained that his parents dressed for dinner and he'd prefer that she didn't wear her jeans. So she had changed, at his request. But her hair was back to being curly and she flat out refused to put more makeup on than mascara and lip gloss.

Was Nick being a royal jerk? Or was he just overreacting because he wanted the evening to go smoothly for her? She wanted to believe it was the latter.

"I know I already told you this," he said as he pulled into a garage beneath his parents' house. "But Mom can be—blunt. Try not to take offense. That's just how she is, and years of us talking to her about it hasn't changed a damn thing."

Dallas put her hand on Nick's leg. "Hey. If she doesn't like me, that's okay—as long as *you* like me."

That seemed to calm his nerves a bit. He leaned over and kissed her lightly on the lips. "I *love* you."

"I love you too." The words rolled off her tongue so easily. Naturally. Truthfully.

She waited for Nick to come around and open her door; he liked to be the gentleman, so, even though she was perfectly capable of opening her own door, she waited for him.

Compromise. Nick had been talking quite a lot about compromise. Until last night, she hadn't known that he was thinking as far ahead for them as marriage. Yes, it had crossed her mind as a fleeting thought—a whim—but she hadn't considered it seriously. Nick, on the other hand, was a planner, and he saw her as a part of his five-year plan.

She loved him—she was *in love* with him—and the idea of finding a way to blend their opposite worlds was an appealing thought. One she wasn't going to reject without serious consideration.

"Let's do this thing." Nick took her hand in his.

It was strange meeting Angus Brand after having known Hank Brand all her life. Angus had so many similar features that he could almost have been Hank's twin—and you could imagine what Hank would have looked like if he hadn't spent his life in the saddle, the harsh Montana sun as his mistress. Angus had receding white hair, much thinner and shorter than Hank's. Angus was, at least at first meeting, quieter than his brother, and much more serious.

Nick's mother was the talker of the two. She talked while she walked, she talked in between directing the many servants milling around the house and she talked rather than eating her meal. Much of what she talked about seemed like mindless jabber to Dallas—this person bought this house, that person was getting divorced from the other person and another couple just bought the most amazing yacht and wouldn't it be great if they upgraded their yacht this year too?

Nick sat stiffly next to her eating quietly for the most part. When he was around his parents, a new Nick appeared. This Nick was stiff as a board and more nervous than a person should be around his parents. Dallas couldn't figure it out, but it just made her feel bad for Nick. Her childhood had been unorthodox and full of upheaval, but she always knew that Davy accepted her as is.

"Dallas—that's an interesting name for a girl." Nick's mother's attention turned from her husband to her guest. "Is that a family name?"

When she said the words *family name*, although nothing in her face changed, her tone of voice sounded like she had just smelled something rotten. So far, Nick's mom had been fairly cordial, if condescending in her expressions. The words that had come out of her mouth were benign. Perhaps she just needed to warm up, because there was a sharp edge to her tone now that felt very much like a pointed barb aimed in Dallas's direction.

"It is— I'm named for my grandpop."

Nick's mom had cut off the tiniest of bits; Dallas didn't know how a person could sustain herself if she put that much energy into just one itty-bitty bite. Nick's mom looked at him with a barely perceptible quirk of her eyebrow, smiling a smile that didn't have a thing to do with being friendly while she chewed.

"How delightful," Nick's mom finally said after she chewed that one little piece of food for so long that Dallas was sure that it had been pulverized. "Do you hear that, Angus? Dallas is named after her grandfather." She laughed as if what she was going to say next was certain to be funny. "I don't think this is going to catch on as a wildfire trend in Chicago…"

"Mom." Nick sent a warning shot over the bow.

"He never wants me to speak to his friends," his mother complained to her. "I should just have my mouth surgically sewn shut. Would that make you happy, Nicholas?"

Dallas put her hand on Nick's knee to let him know that she was holding her own. Compared to living with a bunch of smelly, loudmouthed, raucous and rude cow-pokes, Vivian Brand was a walk in the park.

"What is it that you do, Dallas?" Another false laugh. "I'm having such a hard time with that *name*."

Dallas put her fork down and told Nick's parents about barrel racing, her life on the road, becoming a professional, her aspirations. By the expression on her face, Nick's mom was horrified by what she had just heard; the only reaction out of Angus, whose body was present, but whose mind was generally elsewhere, was when she mentioned Hank. Then Angus's mouth moved from the neutral position downward into a frown, and then he drank a lot of water as if he had to wash a bitter taste out of his mouth.

The false laugh was one of Vivian's favorite weapons, Dallas figured out quickly. After she stopped talking, Nick's mom smiled that tight, condescending smile, laughed in that way that sounded more like an insult and said, "I am sorry—I didn't understand a *word* you just said."

"She has a thick accent," Nick jumped in, in an apparent attempt to shave the tip off that barb. "Sometimes I still don't catch every word."

Dallas's fingers tightened around the stem of her glass; Nick had never once said anything about her thick country twang before tonight. She glanced at Nick, who seemed oblivious of the fact that she might be insulted by his comment. This wasn't the time to discuss the issue with him—the last thing his mother needed was more ammunition.

That set the tone for the rest of the meal. It wasn't hard for her to understand how Nick could be so different than his parents—hadn't she turned out different than hers? Like Nick, she had followed in her father's career footsteps, but that was where the similarities ended. And her mother? Who was she to judge mothers? Her mother had had an affair with a long-distance trucker from Yakima, Washington. When the judge asked Dallas and her brother who they wanted to live with, her brother picked Mom and she picked Dad. Her mom didn't have much nice to say to her after that. Nick couldn't choose his parents any more than she could.

"Well." Nick's mom walked them to the door after dinner. "I hope you enjoy your trip back to Montana. I'm sure you must be anxious to get back to racing around those little barrels."

"Good night, son." Nick's mom's face softened when she pressed her cheek against Nick's face and pursed her lips to make an air-kiss. "We'll talk soon, yes?"

Nick sighed heavily when he sat down behind the wheel of his car. He put his hands on the steering wheel, leaned his head back, closed his eyes for a minute and said, "I'm sorry."

"What for?"

"Mom. What else?" Nick opened his eyes. "She was in rare form tonight. She's my mom and I love her, but—she can be very…socially conscious."

"I don't blame you for what comes out of your Mom's mouth."

"Thank you for that." Nick pushed the ignition button. "It's hard to believe that Aunt Barb and my mom went to the same high school—they grew up together and look how different they are. Night and day."

When they arrived back at the condo, Dallas went straight out to the balcony. She leaned against the railing, closed her eyes and let the breeze brush away the tension of the dinner. The city noises—the car horns and sirens—that had been loud and obnoxious to her ears her first night in Chicago had now faded into the background like a familiar, almost comforting, white noise. In this city, you never felt like you were entirely isolated. There were always people milling about at all hours of the day and night. At home in Montana, there were times when the isolation, the solitariness, of her life had felt crushing.

Nick came up behind her and put his arms around her. "Are you sure you're okay?"

Dallas wasn't entirely okay—but not because of Nick's mother. She had been warned, so it wasn't a surprise. Vivian didn't approve of her dating her son, but the last time she checked, Nick was a grown-ass man. While it would be nice to have parental approval, it certainly wasn't on her short list of important relationship deal breakers. However, she did have some deal breakers. If the person she was dating didn't accept her thick country twang and all—that *was* a definite deal breaker.

"Not entirely, no."

Nick sighed again. "I knew that this night was going to be tough on you. It was tough on me too. I don't want my mom's *issues* to make you doubt the connection *we have*."

Dallas turned in his arms so she could see his face. "Your mom doesn't like me…"

"I don't think that's entirely true…"

"Let's call a spade a spade, Nick." Dallas scooted away from him. They were too close to have a serious conversation. "She doesn't like me. And that's okay."

Nick turned his back to the railing, leaned against

it, loosened his tie and then crossed his arms in front of his body. "But there is a problem."

"I don't see no sense in holdin' things in," Dallas said plainly. "I didn't like what you said about my accent."

Nick seemed perplexed. "Your accent? What did I say?"

"You said that sometimes you don't understand what I say."

"Oh…that. I was just trying to—hell, I don't know what I was trying to do."

"You've never said anything about my accent before." Dallas decided to keep on standing, and now her arms were crossed in front of her body. "I didn't like it."

In fact, it had hurt her feelings, which she almost said, and then changed the words right before they left her mouth.

Nick looked away, out to the city landscape, then down at his crossed feet, while he thought about what she had said.

"I was wrong to say that," Nick admitted. "I'm sorry."

Dallas heard sincerity in his voice—he hadn't meant to hurt her. "I know I *speak country*—I just didn't know it bothered you."

Nick, for the second time in a short while, looked stunned by her words. He dropped his arms, pushed away from the railing and put his hands on her shoulders. "I like your accent, Dallas. It's a part of who you are. And I *love* who you are."

The night that Dallas had met Nick's parents was the first night they didn't make love since they had arrived in Chicago. When they got into bed, she just couldn't muster the desire. She told Nick that she was tired, and she was—exhausted, actually—and he confessed that he was exhausted, as well. But underneath that truth, Dallas knew that part of the reason why she didn't want to make love was the hurtful comment Nick had made about her accent.

She'd been picked on, in one way or another, all her life. Her mother never had a kind word—and even though Davy was a legend, he was a poor legend because he drank, gambled and squandered his money away. There was no "college fund" with her name on it—she was a poor kid who was unsupervised for most of her life—she had to make her own way. And she had made her own way—the best way she knew how. Her skin had gotten pretty thick over the years, so someone like Nick's mom tossing barbs her way didn't sting at all—they bounced off her alligator hide like dull toothpicks. But the rare someone she had let slip behind her tough alligator hide had the power to hurt her tenfold with an offhand comment.

The next day, Nick surprised her by taking half the day off so he could show her a horse facility he'd found in a nearby Chicago suburb. Dallas did have to admit that she was blown away by the fact that there was a place to keep horses so close to a sprawling city.

Nick drove them an hour out of the city to a picturesque country suburb of Chicago named Hampshire. Dallas felt herself immediately start to breathe more slowly in the country—it was beyond her imagination that land this tranquil and sparsely populated was an hour drive away from the city center.

"What do you think?" Nick asked her.

"I love it out here." She had rolled her window down

and was enjoying the feel of the fresh air on her face. "I can *breathe* out here."

Nick laughed. "I breathe just fine in the city."

Dallas reached over and put her hand on his leg. Nick taking time off from work was a major deal for him— and for him to make a plan to get her out of the city was exactly the kind of thoughtfulness that made her fall in love with him a little bit more each day.

"That's 'cuz you're a city mouse and I'm a country mouse."

Dallas leaned her head back with a happy smile. The fewer people and more land she saw, the better she felt. And, as a bonus, she actually saw *horses*! An hour out of downtown Chicago, *horses*! And pasture. It made her feel like she wasn't in a foreign land after all—there had to be at least one or two of her peeps out here in the burbs.

"I think this is it." Nick slowed his car when the GPS indicated that his turn was a few feet ahead.

"What is it?"

"The place I wanted to show you."

Dallas sat upright and put her hands on the dash when she saw a large sign for an equestrian center. It was then that Dallas knew exactly why Nick had brought her out to the suburban countryside: he wanted to show her how she could live near Chicago while still training for her barrel racing competitions.

"Keep an open mind," Nick said when he parked the car.

"Trust me." Dallas leaned over to give a quick kiss. "My mind is *wide*-open."

Nick loved watching Dallas at the stable, particularly when she spotted someone training their horse in a Western saddle, wearing a cowboy hat! His plan was to show Dallas that, if their relationship progressed as he hoped it would, she didn't have to give up her horses or her training. In fact, he believed that he could help her reach her goal of earning enough money to qualify for the NFR in Las Vegas. What she needed was an infusion of sponsorship money—that money could be used to buy an extra horse so she could rotate Blue out, give him time to rest, while she kept right on competing. The sponsorship money could go to buying a new rig, traveling expenses—he'd also noticed that some of the top contenders, the women who were on their way to NFR this year, had assistants. Why shouldn't Dallas? God knew she had all the talent she needed. She was Davy Dalton's daughter, and it showed—she had his gift with horses, his charisma when it counted and his competitive spirit. Nick had seen Dallas's magnetic appeal—heck, he had fallen under her spell right away—she had that undeniable, intangible "it" factor that made a star a star.

"Ah!" Dallas slumped into the passenger seat with a contented smile on her face. "I love this place! The facilities, the arenas—the *indoor* arena so I can keep on trainin' right through the winter. Plenty of pasture for turnout."

Nick loved to watch her face when she spoke about her passion and her profession—her face flushed a pretty shade of rosy pink, her eyes sparkled.

"And they ride Western here too! I didn't expect that *at all*. Not at all."

He had expected it. He had picked this facility specifically because it was the only one that catered to both English and Western riders.

"Oh…" Dallas sighed happily. "Don't you just love the smell of hay and manure?"

Nick clicked his seat belt with a shake of his head. "No. I can't say that I do."

That night, they were back on track. They shed their clothing and met each other halfway at the center of the bed. Facing each other, their arms and legs intertwined, their bodies connected, they kissed and murmured sounds of pleasure and words of love as they found their rhythm. It was like an intimate dance, so close, so passionate—their bodies were pressed tightly together as if they didn't want to have any distance between them. Nick rolled Dallas onto her back, keeping their bodies connected, braced his feet on the bed and thrust into her, deeper, harder, until she was gasping in his arms, clawing her fingernails down his back.

"Yes, baby." Nick kissed her neck. "Come for me."

Dallas writhed beneath him, pushing against his groin, wanting more of him, wanting all of him. He held her tight, the muscles in his arms tense and hurting, but he didn't let her go until she had stilled beneath him. Her face and neck and hairline were damp with perspiration. He kissed her face—her forehead, her eyes, her lips.

"I love you, baby," he murmured against her lips.

Dallas wrapped one leg around his back and they rolled together, still connected, always connected, until he was on his back and she was straddling him. The look on her face when she began to move up and down his hard shaft almost made him climax on the spot. Sheer control; sheer desire.

His cowgirl rode him slow and deep, bracing her

hands on his abdomen, pushing down on him; he held on to her healthy hips, digging his fingers into her flesh, guiding her body back and forth until he felt himself begin to climax. She knew his sound—that sound he made when his body was ready for that ephemeral wave of ecstasy. Dallas leaned back, put her arms behind her and rested them on his thighs.

Nick was mesmerized by the beauty of the sexy woman loving him—watching her, her head back, her small breasts, the tips of her hair brushing across the tops of his thighs.

"Ahhhhh!" Nick bucked upward as he climaxed.

It was such a powerful orgasm that it felt like he could have blown right through that condom. In his mind, he kept on wanting to rip off that condom, shove himself deep inside Dallas and pump her full of his seed. The more he thought about getting Dallas pregnant, the hotter he'd gotten.

Dallas collapsed forward to rest before they uncoupled their bodies. She kissed his bare chest and then kissed his lips.

"I love you too, Nick."

"I know you do, baby." Nick brushed her hair off her back and held her close for one minute more. "I feel it."

Chapter Fourteen

The equestrian farm was for Dallas. Today was for him. He'd been waiting all week to take Dallas out on his family's yacht and show her Lake Michigan. This was *his* lake—the only thing he loved more than practicing law was being out on the lake with his friends. He wanted Dallas to feel the way he did about the lake— he wanted her to fit seamlessly into his group of "lake bums" who had been swimming or boating Lake Michigan since they were all kids. They had grown up together on this lake. In a way, the waters of this great lake were his second home.

His family's yacht club, Chicago Yacht Club, was a short fifteen minutes away from his condo. His life, his work life, his play life, had always been a small circumference. That was how he liked it. If he moved out to the suburbs with Dallas, if their relationship progressed to a more committed level, he would have to give up his easy access to Lake Michigan and would have to commute to work.

"Here she is," Nick said proudly of the sleek white-

and-silver yacht in the sloop. His father had named the yacht *Amicus Curiae*, translated from Latin: *Friend of the Court*.

"Do you like her?" he asked when she didn't say anything.

"Absolutely, I do."

Nick ensured that she boarded the yacht safely; they walked up four narrow steps to the main deck of the yacht.

"Do you drive this monster?" she asked him.

"Since I was twelve." He put his gear on an L-shaped couch located on the main deck.

Dallas spun around the large living room area that included several sitting areas, a dining area and a staircase leading down to the lower deck.

"I'll take you topside in a minute—but I want to show you the bedrooms and the kitchen."

Nick led Dallas down the narrow staircase to the four cabins below. The master bedroom was a large room that allowed for a queen-size bed, a roomy bathroom with a shower and a cozy sitting area that could be used as a reading nook, a game table or a place to have an intimate dinner away from guests.

"This's bigger than the house I grew up in," Dallas noted. "Heck, this boat—"

"Yacht."

"Boat. Yacht. Whatever you call it, it's bigger than my place *now*."

Nick hugged her with a smile. "I've been waiting for this day all week. I love being on the water as much as you love racing."

He took her topside—there was as open-air captain's chair with a copilot seat, a place to sunbathe at the front of the yacht and a banquet for eating, drinking and merrymaking.

"Make yourself at home," Nick said. "I've got to hit the checklist before everyone starts to arrive. I want to be able to get out on the water as soon as the gang's aboard."

Dallas sat down at the outdoor banquet on the top-side while Nick took care of his presailing checklist. Every once in a while, Nick would catch her eye and smile at her. Even when he was going about his business, he was worried about her comfort. No man in her life, not even her father, had ever spent so much of his time making sure that *she* was okay. It was refreshing, frightening and hard to trust. But, then again, she had difficulty with trust in general.

"Jordan's comin' today, right?" she asked.

Nick looked up from his task on the starboard side of the yacht. "As far as I know."

"Is her husband comin' with her?"

"No. He had to go back to San Diego—Jordan stayed behind to close the exhibit."

Dallas was relieved that Jordan was coming on this outing—the idea of being stuck on a boat, even a roomy one like this, with all Nick's friends and colleagues made her skin itch. She wasn't really much of a people person, and she *really* wasn't much of a fan of the "upper crust." There were plenty of people in barrel racing who had loads more money than common sense or common decency. Money didn't make the man or woman, and sometimes it turned people rotten. Now, maybe she was rushing to judgment with Nick's friends from his yacht and country club—after all, he had shed much of his elitism instilled in him by his mother—so she was open to them proving her wrong.

Either way, Jordan would be a friendly face from home as well as an ally in a crowd of strangers. Unfortunately, Jordan, who had a reputation for being unfashionably late, had to call Nick and tell him to hold the yacht. By then, twenty of Nick's friends, male and female, had arrived and had truly made themselves at home on the *Amicus Curiae*. The comfort level of all Nick's friends on the family yacht gave Dallas an inkling as to how often this gang got together to party on Lake Michigan.

"Nicky!" Dallas heard Jordan's voice from her perch on the cocaptain's chair on the sundeck. "Dallas!"

Dallas hopped off the white cushioned chair and leaned over the deck railing so she could wave at Nick's cousin.

Jordan, thankfully, seemed as out of step with Nick's friends as she was—Jordan was wearing black cigarette pants, a black ribbed tank that showed off two tattooed arm cuffs on each of her biceps. She had large sunglasses on, and her lavender hair looked a deeper shade of purple in the bright sun. Jordan looked like she had stepped out of a rock-and-roll magazine, just as much as she looked like she stepped out of a calendar for John Deere tractor.

"Sweet baby Jesus, Mary and Joseph!" Jordan stopped on the top step that led up to the sundeck with dramatic flair. "I thought I'd missed the boat, for sure."

"You've missed something," Nick teased her.

"Ha-ha, coz." Jordan hugged her cousin. "I'm here so you can drop anchor or shove off or whatever is appropriate for a mammoth vessel such as this."

Jordan pulled up her sunglasses so Dallas could see her wink before she dropped the glasses back down over her Brand-blue eyes. As she hugged Dallas, she said, "You've got to keep the Brand men in check, Dallas, so they're clear who's boss."

"I'm so glad you're here." Dallas hugged Jordan back, probably a little tighter than she needed to—but after the brief time spent with Nick's friends, Dallas felt like she needed two things: a life vest in case she needed to abandon ship and Jordan to stop her from jumping overboard.

Dallas didn't want to think that his friends were awful—but they *were* awful. They all came with baggage, and not just carry-on. Although they all had plenty of that. They came with expensive designer bags that they tossed around and dropped on the deck as if they were cloth sacks from the thrift store. The women were in full regalia, even though they were supposed to be ready for a day in the sun. Their makeup was done, tasteful, but noticeable. They had all their jewelry on display, designer sunglasses, the works. They were wearing high heels—on a yacht! How smart was that? Now, some of them had been very friendly, but the conversation had fizzled out soon after the introductions because they only had Nick in common. Others were just as snotty and elitist as Nick's mother.

"That good, huh?" Jordan said, apparently picking up on the meaning behind the death-grip hug.

"Yeah…" Jordan continued as she looked around at the crowd. "That's about right."

Jordan held up her ivory-white arms and added, "This skin does not do sun, so when you get tired of flirting with the captain, come find me."

For the first part of the trip on Lake Michigan, Dallas forgot about Nick's friends and focused on the scenery of the great lake and on Captain Brand. It was sunny and breezy, the yacht cut through the water like a dream and Dallas was having one of the best times of her trip to Chicago. This was in part because watching Nick captaining the yacht, sharing one of his loves with her, was so much fun. Nick looked every bit the preppy young professional with nicely cut shorts, a sapphire-blue short-sleeve button-down with UV protection built-in and slip-resistant boat shoes without socks. She had never realized that preppy could be so sexy—but it was definitely sexy on Nick.

"Are you loving this?" Nick smiled at her, his hands steady on the wheel.

She nodded and returned his smile.

"I'm glad you're here," Nick said for the second time that day.

"Me too," Dallas replied, and meant it wholeheartedly.

At least for the next thirty minutes.

"How is she?" Nick had left his captain's perch to check on her belowdecks in the master bedroom.

Dallas saw Jordan hitch her thumb toward the bathroom as she opened the door. She shut the door behind her, her hand on her churning stomach.

"I'm glad I had a small breakfast," she answered.

As they were known to do, the water conditions on Lake Michigan had turned choppy and rough, and that rocking motion had introduced her to seasickness.

"Oh, baby—you don't look so good."

It was the truth and she knew it. Her face, which typically had a nice healthy color, had a yellowish-green undertone. She was so seasick that she had lost her breakfast, and thanked the sea gods that she hadn't had a chance to eat any of the food that was on board.

"Here." Nick pulled the covers back on the bed. "See if lying down will help."

Sitting on the edge of the bed, her stomach feeling sicker than when she had the flu, Dallas was grateful at how kind Nick was being about her getting sick. Nick helped her pull off her boots before he helped her lean back.

"Who's steering the boat?" Dallas asked with a froglike hoarse voice.

"Yacht," he corrected teasingly.

He brushed her hair off her forehead. "I'm going to turn around and head back."

"You don't have to do that," she protested.

"I can't have a good time knowing you're down here feeling lousy," he said with concerned eyes. "Besides, not having you up there with me is taking some of the fun out of it for me."

Jordan promised to stay with her while Nick cut the trip short and headed back to shore.

"That Nick, he's all right." Jordan was lying on top of the covers beside her.

"He is."

"I don't know *what* he sees in that group up there. There's only one or two I'd be willing to toss a lifesaver to if they fell overboard."

Dallas gave a laugh for a second, which ended with a groan.

Jordan looked at her. "Well, it's true. Grandma Brand would call them all a bunch of phony baloneys."

"My pappy would call them all a bunch of heifers in houndstooth. I never knew what that meant, but I knew what it *meant*."

"Do you know one of them actually asked me if I got my skin bleached? I wanted to slap her right off the boat," Jordan said with a laugh.

"Yacht."

"Whatever." Her new friend added, "And if I heard one more of them call your accent *adorable*…"

"I know. I can tell most of them think I'm as dumb as a dirt farmer."

"Well—Nick proved that he could spot quality when he decided to take you off the market."

"Thank you…"

"You're welcome. Now all he needs is to start seriously thinning the herd—"

"Preach."

"—and *we kicked it in high school* shouldn't be the only criteria for making the cut."

The day he'd planned on Lake Michigan didn't turn out exactly how he'd imagined it. He had wanted to have time to circulate through his friends with Dallas on his arm in order to integrate these two separate components of his life together. Dallas spent all her time, preseasickness, as his copilot and he loved the time they had shared—that was a highlight. But when she did get seasick, the opportunity for her to get to know his friends was cut short.

Next time.

"What looks good to you?" He put his menu down on the table.

For their last "nonpacking" night of Dallas's trip to

Chicago, Nick wanted to honor her love for a high-rise view and take her to the Signature Room, located on the ninety-fifth floor of the John Hancock Building. He was rewarded with delight in her soft hazel eyes and a squeeze of his hand when they were waiting for the hostess to seat them at the table he had reserved for them; he wanted to make sure that Dallas got one of the best seats in the house. She deserved it.

"I think I'm gonna join you in that surf and turf," she said. "You made it sound so good when you talked about it."

Nick ordered them both the surf and turf. He wanted to broach a subject with Dallas that she had skillfully avoided the entire time they were in Chicago. As he got to know her better, he was beginning to see that Dallas did not like to discuss future plans. She liked to take life as it came—one day at a time—while he had a five-year and a ten-year plan in place already. He'd done enough "free floating" after college, and all that had gotten him, in his opinion, was really far behind in the race of life. So many of his college friends were partners, or had sold their start-up companies and were on to the next venture. He'd be playing catch-up with his more focused contemporaries for the rest of his life. The only thing that he wasn't behind in—in his opinion—was the wife and kids. That was variable, and he never felt rushed in that department.

Now that he had found Dallas, he'd like to begin to pin that part of his life down. Now, of course, they had to continue to get to know each other—a long-distance relationship could actually force them to slow down and really learn to communicate—but he already felt in his gut that he'd found his wife. He just knew it. Getting her on board with his gut feeling was proving to be more challenging than expected.

"I'm sorry you didn't have a chance to get to spend more time getting to know my friends," he said.

Dallas tried not to give away every emotion she had regarding his friends in her expression; she had already shared with him that she didn't think she had enough in common with them, other than him, to feel a connection.

"Next time," he added.

Nick reached over to take her hand in his. "You look so pretty in that dress, Dallas."

"I'm glad I got a chance to wear it again before it ends up in a ball at the bottom of my suitcase," she said of the black cocktail dress she had worn the night of the symphony.

"Cocktail dresses suit you."

Dallas took a sip of water with a wrinkle in her brow. "I don't mind every now and again."

A couple of times Nick had tried to get Dallas to change her wardrobe while she was in the city; he even offered to take her shopping. But she was stubborn about comfort. She wanted to wear her cowgirl boots, jeans in varying shades of blue and, always, her cowgirl hat. He loved her—he knew he did—and yet her cowgirl wardrobe in Chicago bothered him. It was difficult for him to justify those two different positions. He'd never had to deal with that before, and he still wasn't exactly sure how to be okay with it now.

"So." Nick changed the subject. "What are your thoughts about that equestrian center in Hampshire?"

Dallas buttered a piece of bread and handed it to him as she always did. "I loved it."

"If our relationship progressed."

The cowgirl looked up from her chore of buttering another piece of bread.

He continued, "Can you see yourself training there?"

Deep in thought, Dallas finished buttering her bread, put the bread uneaten on her plate and dusted the crumbs off her fingers.

"I think," Dallas said seriously, "that I could."

That was a substantial move in the right direction.

"I also think it's still pretty soon to be worryin' too much about it." Dallas's brow was furrowed, a sign that she took the subject very seriously.

"I know you do. But my career path is here, not in Montana. That's as nonnegotiable for me as your barrel racing is for you. Your career gives you more flexibility, if you're willing. If you can't see yourself living in a place like Hampshire, I'm afraid we'd be dead in the water." Nick looked at her intently. "I don't want that."

Dallas had taken a bite of her bread; she chewed, swallowed, then asked, "And you'd be happy with an hour commute? We've hardly left a five-mile radius all week. Your whole life is right here downtown."

"I've thought long and hard about that, Dallas. I love living downtown—being close to work and close to the lake. But to be able to build a life with you—maybe start a family—I'd make the burbs work."

After dinner, they had walked downtown to walk off their dinner. Her first night in Chicago had been overwhelming; it was so noisy and crowded and there were unusual smells that were sometimes pleasant and sometimes *not so* pleasant. Tonight, she felt as if she had begun a bit of a love affair with Nick's hometown.

The city was *alive* in a way that was tangible; Dallas had begun to love the feeling of that energy and constant movement. And even though she'd gotten seasick, she had definitely seen the appeal of Lake Michigan. A lake so large that could be as wild and unpredictable as an ocean was a thing of beauty. She had introduced Nick to her favorite lake in Montana, and now Nick had been able to introduce her to his.

After their walk, they returned to Nick's condo; after drinking a glass of wine on the balcony, they met each other in the middle of his bed and made love. Their lovemaking was more slow and tender, as if they knew that soon they wouldn't be able express their love for each other in that way. She had only one more day in Chicago, but Nick had to work. So this was their last full day together on this trip. Soon, she would return to Montana to train and get back to racing. And he would get back to the routine of his life without her.

"Don't move yet." Nick kissed her on the lips.

Their bodies were facing each other, their limbs intertwined; he was still inside her, but not as hard after he had just climaxed. Their skin was damp with perspiration; the bedsheets were damp from their lovemaking.

"Dallas…" He pushed her hair away from her face. "Dallas… I love you so much."

"I love you." She felt him slip out of her body.

Nick rolled her onto her back and moved on top of her so he was looking down at her face. "Let's make this work between us."

"I want it to."

She did want this relationship to work with Nick. Did she think they made perfect sense? No. But that was part of what she liked about it. They challenged each other—they helped each other grow. It was never going to be dull between them, that was almost a certainty.

She reached up and touched his face. "I'm gonna miss you, Nick."

Nick turned his face and kissed the palm of her hand. "I'm going to miss you. Way too much."

Chapter Fifteen

Dallas woke up late, barely remembering Nick kissing her goodbye before he headed off to work. This was her last day in Chicago—tonight they had planned to order room service from the hotel and stay in. She planned on getting herself packed during her alone time so she didn't have to waste her last moments with Nick stuffing her dirty socks into her suitcase.

The week in Chicago had been eye-opening and wonderful; Nick had wined and dined her and was very conscientious about the activities he chose. He kept her likes, her wants, her needs at the forefront of his mind when he planned their week together. She wanted to do something for him. He was always surprising her—she wanted to return the favor.

"I'm late." Dallas looked at the time on her phone.

She used the remote control on the nightstand to open the light-blocking curtains. The late-morning light streamed into the room, making Dallas squint.

"That's too bright," the cowgirl muttered. It had taken her hours to fall asleep the night before. After they made love, Nick had fallen asleep promptly—the man had a knack for falling asleep almost on demand—while she had tossed, turned, stared at the ceiling, until she finally got up and went out into the living room.

The conversation Nick had initiated at the restaurant had flustered her. She hadn't expected to fall in love with a Chicago attorney who aspired to be a state supreme court judge. Yes, Nick checked so many of the boxes for a man she had imaged could flesh out her already full life. He was hardworking, educated, sophisticated. Perhaps they didn't make much sense on paper, considering her upbringing, her own style and her chosen lifestyle, but she actually loved his clean, preppy, country-club look. To her, it was sexy.

But move to a Chicago suburb? That was around fifteen hundred miles off course. It had never occurred to her that she would live anywhere other than Montana. Not once. She could move—of course she could move—but did she *want* to change the image of her future life she had always had in her head? If her relationship with Nick continued to flourish? After a sleepless night of the wheels spinning in her brain, she had landed on a tentative yes.

The long, hot shower, where her skin came out red and her fingers were pruned, made her feel more awake. She got dressed, checked the time, found the menu for the hotel restaurant and then ordered Nick's favorite lunchtime fare, to go. Even though he had told her to spoil herself at the spa and rest for her trip home, she had decided to go with a different activity: a surprise picnic lunch for Nick. After all, a young lawyer on the upwardly mobile trajectory had to eat, didn't he?

Dallas felt proud of herself; it wasn't like her to "surprise" men with a romantic gesture like the one she had planned for Nick. She had questioned him about his favorite items on the menu, she had purchased a card that could be categorized as "mushy," and she had figured out how to best get herself, the food and the card to his downtown law office without him ever suspecting her. The man had really brought her out of her shell—he had allowed her to tap in to a more sensitive side of her personality that she kind of liked.

"Howdy," Dallas said to the receptionist in the navy-blue suit. "I'm here to see Nick Brand."

The receptionist gave her a studied smile, picked up the phone on the desk and pushed a button. "Hi. Mr. Brand. Did you order some food?"

Dallas waved her hand to get the receptionist's attention. "No. I'm here to see him."

The receptionist held her hand over the lower part of the phone. "I'm so sorry—I just assumed. Do you have an appointment?"

"Just tell him that Dallas's waitin' for him," she said. "I'll wait right over here."

"I'm sorry, Mr. Brand. A Dallas is here to see you? I don't think she has an appointment."

The receptionist hung up and said, "Mr. Brand will be right with you."

She was nervous. *Nervous* to be putting herself out there—and writing down how much Nick's kindness and caring, from the very beginning, had meant to her.

She heard Nick's voice before she saw him. Dallas stood up, excited to see Nick with his attorney hat on. But when Nick came around the corner and into the reception room, the tense, almost irritated expression on his face immediately took the wind right out of her sails. He didn't even smile at her.

"What are you doing here?" Nick put his hand on her back to turn her toward the door.

Put off by his cold greeting, Dallas held up the bag in her hand. "Surprising you."

"Karen—let Mr. Conner know that I'll be right back," Nick told the receptionist as he held the door open for Dallas.

Outside in the hallway, Nick said, his face tense, "I thought you were going to go to the spa?"

His obvious discomfort with her at his workplace wiped the smile right off her face.

"Again—I wanted to surprise you with lunch."

"Thank you." Nick glanced at the bag in her hand. "I appreciate the thought."

He didn't *look* like he appreciated the thought. He looked like he wanted to shove her onto the elevator as quickly as he could. Of all the reactions she had anticipated, this reaction wasn't anywhere on her radar.

"Here." Dallas handed him the bag. "For when you get a free minute."

Nick took the bag from her; the card was still in the bag and she almost reached in there and took it back. But she meant every word she had written. And maybe Nick was having a bad day—maybe he was getting chewed out by *Mr. Connor*. Shouldn't she give him the benefit of the doubt?

Nick walked beside her along the corridor that lead to the elevator. "I'm sorry, Dallas. I'm right in the middle of a meeting."

She tried to cover her disappointment and felt that

she failed pretty miserably. She had never been good at pretending. Not even when she was a kid.

When the elevator dinged she said, "I hope your day ends better than it started."

Nick reached for her hand—the tension on his face had softened a bit. "It will end better because I will be with you."

They kissed a brief kiss before she got on the elevator. As the doors slid shut quietly, Nick gave her a quick wave, then headed back to his workday. Dallas felt deflated as she walked alone back to the condo. The walk didn't help her outlook—it actually gave her time to mull things over in her mind and by the time she walked through the condo door, she had concluded something about her brief interaction with Nick: he had been anxious by her appearance at his office—he had been *embarrassed*.

Nick was embarrassed of *her*.

Nick had done his best to focus on his work after Dallas left. His reaction to seeing her in his law firm, dressed in her country best, had been *uncensored*. Dallas had to have seen how uncomfortable he was because it had been obvious in his expression. If he hadn't already felt like a world-class heel, he certainly did when he found the card she had taped to his favorite sandwich. She had put some thought into the surprise and he had stomped all over it. And he had a feeling that their last night together before she headed back to Montana was not going to be a good one.

"Dallas?" Nick walked into the condo and followed his normal routine of dropping his keys on the side table along with his mail. "I'm home."

Dallas had begun a ritual of coming out from wherever she was in the condo and meeting him at the end of the entryway. Tonight, she had opted to end that ritual. He found her out on the balcony. She was sitting in the dark, staring out at the skyscrapers, pensive.

"It's another beautiful night." Nick unbuttoned his suit jacket and sat down beside her.

"I am going to really miss this view," Dallas said quietly.

There was an invisible wall between them now—he had worked really hard to gain her trust, and perhaps he hadn't wrecked it completely, but he had damaged it.

"I loved the card, Dallas." He took her hand in his; she didn't pull away, so he knew that the wound he had inflicted wasn't a fatal wound. But he had hurt her. He knew he had.

"I'm sorry I ruined your surprise. It was…" He sighed. "It was a tough day."

"Don't." She slipped her hand out of his and put it in her lap.

She looked at him then. "Don't cover it up."

Nick's heart started to pound at her words. The tone of her voice made him rethink his immediate assessment of the damage—it was much worse than he had thought. Much worse.

"Okay…" Nick stood up, took off his suit jacket, pulled his tie off and unbuttoned the top buttons of his shirt. "Tell me what's on your mind, Dallas. I don't want our trip to end with us at odds. How can I make this better?"

Dallas was quiet for an extended pause, and then she said to him, "I embarrass you."

Nick had pulled his chair closer to hers and turned it toward her so he could face her while they talked. "No."

In the soft yellow light, she met his eyes. "Yes. I embarrass you. The way I talk, my clothes. I embarrass you."

"Jesus, Dallas—don't go blowing one little thing all out of whack. I was having a bad day—you caught me at a bad moment—that's all."

"All week, I've seen you cringe at some of the things I say—or how I say them. You've asked me to not wear my hat. You wanted to take me shopping for Chicago clothes."

"Are you really going to go there? We've had an amazing time together, and now you're going to pick it apart? Why?"

Dallas stood up and went inside the condo. He followed her.

"This is who I am, Nick." Dallas was standing in his living room now. "I like my hat and my boots—I'm always gonna wear jeans rather than a dress, I'm gonna drive a truck and I talk country."

Nick threw his jacket and tie onto a nearby chair. "You're looking pretty hard for problems, Dallas."

He took a step closer to her; he could feel her walling him off, word by word, brick by brick.

"No," Dallas said in a monotone voice. "I didn't go lookin' for this problem. This problem? This problem is all you."

Her simple statement caught him off guard. But it was the tone of her voice that really had him worried. She didn't sound like his girl anymore. Her voice was flat, almost emotionless.

"You need to be honest with me, Nick," Dallas continued. "Tell me the truth. Do I embarrass you?"

Nick sighed heavily and rubbed his hands over his face several times. She had him backed into a corner and there was only one way out: tell the truth.

"I don't ever want to hurt you, Dallas," he started.

Dallas felt her stomach start to churn; it already hurt, thinking that the man she loved, the man she had let into her private world, was embarrassed by her.

Dallas wrapped her arms tightly in front of her body. "Too late."

It was a shame that their trip had ended on such a bad note. But it had. Dallas went back to her life on the rodeo circuit, chasing her dream to earn enough points to make it to the big show in Las Vegas. And he spent his time working as hard as he could to prove himself to the partners at the firm. He wanted them to come to respect his drive, his knowledge of the law and his work ethic. As busy as he was, Dallas was never far from his mind.

They hadn't completely severed their relationship; they kept in touch by phone and text and email. Nick always watched any of her races on YouTube; it helped him feel connected to her. He still loved Dallas—he was still *in love* with Dallas. And he believed—had to believe—that she still loved him. He had screwed up with her, he knew that. Dallas had made him realize that he had a little too much of his mother in him. Ever since Dallas walked out of his life, he'd been doing some major soul-searching. He loved Dallas—he loved her heart and her passion and her loyalty. If she wanted to walk the Magnificent Mile in a flour sack, he'd walk proudly beside her. Hands down, she was the best thing that had happened to him and he wasn't going to give up until he'd proved to her that he'd changed. He was determined to win the cowgirl back.

Two months had passed since her trip to Chicago—two long months without being able to hold her, or kiss her or make love to her. Every time he tried to make plans to meet her at one of her events, work would suck up his free time on the weekend. After that horrible conversation when he admitted that *at times* she embarrassed him, he hadn't had a chance to see her in person—to try to mend fences. As much as he had seen the genuine hurt in her eyes that last night they shared, he hurt. He hurt because he had hurt the woman he loved. And until he made it right with her, he supposed he would just keep on hurting.

Dallas is coming to Bent Tree for Thanksgiving. Are you?

Nick stopped typing the email he was composing to read the text he had just received from his cousin Jordan. Barbara was planning a big family Thanksgiving at the ranch; she had invited him, but he hadn't been able give her a definitive "yeah" or "nah" because of the grunt cases the firm had been piling on his desk. It wasn't glamorous being the low man on the totem pole of a large firm. Most of the time he felt like a highly paid gofer.

Nick stared at his phone. Dallas at Bent Tree for Thanksgiving. This would be the perfect time and place to finally get her face-to-face so he could apologize. He wasn't opposed to a little groveling if it came to that.

Nick used his thumbs to text a quick message back to Jordan: Tell Aunt Barb to count me in for Thanksgiving.

He was going to Montana for Thanksgiving to try to earn back the trust of his woman. Now all he had to do was come up with a gesture—a really big, hard-to-resist gesture.

"Barb? Are you back here?"

Dallas had been back at Bent Tree for a couple of weeks. Bessy the Bronco had limped her way to her last rodeo and died. Clint had come to haul Blue back to the ranch, and for the time being she was borrowing one of the Bent Tree's work trucks.

Barbara was sitting on the edge of her bed, holding a small framed picture in her hand. There were tears on her cheeks—Dallas had inadvertently interrupted a private moment. She turned away from the doorway, but Barbara stopped her.

"It's okay, Dallas. You can come in."

Dallas wasn't sure that she *wanted* to come in. Other people's emotions had always made her uncomfortable as much as her own emotions did sometimes. "I just wanted to know if you needed somethin' from the store."

Barbara put the frame on her nightstand; she plucked a tissue from a tissue box next to the lamp and dabbed the tears from her cheeks.

"Thanksgiving was Daniel's favorite holiday," Barbara said.

Daniel was the Brands' second-oldest son, and Luke's twin; Daniel had died in Iraq several years ago, but Dallas could tell that Barbara hadn't fully recovered from the loss. She couldn't even imagine the pain of losing child.

"Okay." Barbara stood up with a little nod. "Let me make you a list."

Dallas created an electronic list on her phone while Barbara went through the menu for Thanksgiving. This year was going to be an epic year for Barbara—for the first time, all of her children were coming to the ranch for Thanksgiving.

"So—let me count the adults first." Barbara slipped on her reading glasses to look at her guest list. "Luke, Sophia, Tyler, London, Jordan, Ian, Josephine, Logan, Taylor, Clint, Brock, Casey, Nick and Dallas."

Dallas's stomach clenched when Barbara read Nick's name. "Nick's comin'?"

Barbara slid her glasses up to the top of her head. "He didn't tell you?"

A wave of nerves swept over her body at the thought of seeing Nick again. She swallowed hard twice and tried to keep her expression neutral when she said, "Not yet."

Dallas had avoided talking about specifics of her relationship with Nick to his family members. Barbara didn't know that her relationship with Nick had been strained for several months. No one did. Barbara moved on because her mind was occupied with Thanksgiving planning. "Counting adults and children, we need enough food for twenty-two people!"

"I have a feelin' I'm gonna be runnin' back and forth to that store a lot," Dallas forecasted.

"You are going to be such a help to me, Dallas." Barbara started to systematically inventory her cabinets, her refrigerator and her pantry.

"Barb? Do you mind if I ask you somethin'?"

"Of course you can."

"How did you adjust to livin' on a ranch? You grew up in Chicago, didn't you?"

"Add shaved coconut to the list, will you?" Barbara shut one of her upper cabinets. Then the matriarch of the Bent Tree Brands joined her at the table. "You must be seeing parallels between my relationship with Hank and your relationship with Nick, right?"

Dallas nodded. "You've made it work."

Barbara laughed. "That's because I love that man more than I love anything else in this world. That's the only way *this*," she said of the ranch, "was ever going to work."

Dallas waited for her to continue; Barbara and Hank Brand seemed as unlikely as Nick and Dallas, but they had been married for over forty years.

"It has not been easy." Barbara was honest with her. "I was so homesick for the city—I missed shopping and restaurants and dry cleaning. It took me *years* to get used to the smell of cow manure and it took me years to get used to the fact that I had married a rancher. I had fallen in love with a rancher, but being the *wife* of a rancher was an adjustment."

Like being the wife of a Chicago lawyer would be an adjustment.

"You made it work." Dallas said her thought aloud.

"We made it work," Barbara agreed. "Because we loved each other. We had to learn to accept our differences—we had to learn to respect them. And yes, I had to choose to give up my life in Chicago to live on a cattle ranch with Hank, a decision I have never regretted. So, if you and Nick love each other, it doesn't really matter if you're in Montana or in Chicago—all that matters is that you are *together*."

Chapter Sixteen

The week before Thanksgiving, Dallas tried not to dwell on her impending reunion with Nick. Helping Barb prepare for her large family gathering kept her too busy, but she still had to work at not playing out scenarios in her head. Sometimes she wanted to tell him off and break things off for good; sometimes she wanted to forgive him and start anew.

As Thanksgiving approached, a new wave of Brand family members was arriving at the ranch each day. Tyler and his wife, London, had arrived from Virginia with their baby daughter, Maggie, and London's teenage son, J.T. Barbara was particularly excited about Tyler returning to the ranch after an extended stay in Virginia to iron out custody issues with J.T.'s father. London had won full custody, as well as the right to live with J.T. in Montana. Their return to the ranch had brought a new excitement and energy to the main house.

Luke and his wife, Sophia, recently reconciled after some time apart, had begun to bring their three young children to the ranch regularly so they could make up for lost time with Tyler and London. The house already seemed so loud and full, and most of the people hadn't arrived. Dallas was grateful to be included, but it was a little overwhelming to have so many people talking all at the same time. Whenever it got too loud for her, Dallas would escape to the barn to spend some time with Blue. Instead of returning to the tree house after her last rodeo, she had taken up residence in the efficiency apartment in the foaling barn usually reserved for interns from the University of Montana.

"Hi, good-looking boy." Dallas wrapped her arms around Blue's warm neck.

Winter was upon them in Montana; the snow that had already coated the mountain peaks in September and October had begun to cover the valleys, as well. It was so cold that Blue's breath, like hers, came out in wispy white puffs.

"They aren't Montana wildflowers, but they're for you."

She had been so absorbed with Blue that she hadn't noticed Nick walk into the barn.

Dressed in Western winter gear—jeans, cowboy boots, a heavy tan coat with a sheepskin collar and her father's cowboy hat—Nick was holding a small bundle of flowers in his hands.

"God, Dallas. You're a sight for sore eyes." Nick's voice cracked a bit. She didn't know if she was ready to forgive him, but she couldn't deny that she could hear how sincerely sorry he was for how things ended between them in Chicago.

Dallas continued to rub the spot between Blue's eyes,

his favorite spot that made his eyes droop, to keep her hands busy. She knew it didn't show on the outside, but the minute she saw Nick, she had the urge to run to him and throw her arms around him. She had pushed aside her feelings in order to focus on competing; she hadn't realized, until just this moment, how much she had really missed him.

"Dallas." Nick took a step closer to her. "Please."

Dallas turned toward him, her arms crossed in front of her chest.

Nick took another step closer to her, approaching her like he would approach a wild horse. Slow and steady.

"I'm sorry." He caught her eyes with his. "I hurt you and I'm sorry."

She could see how sorry Nick was, but did that change anything? She was still a cowgirl from Montana and he was a preppy lawyer from Chicago. Oil and water.

Nick could see that he wasn't getting through to her. Desperate times required desperate measures. He did something that he thought he'd never do—he got down on one knee in front of his love and asked for her forgiveness.

"I love you, Dallas," Nick said in a raw voice. "Forgive me."

Dallas frowned at him for several seconds before she took his flower offering.

"For Pete's sake, Nick. Get up!"

Nick stood up and took another step forward. "Say you forgive me, Dallas."

Dallas smelled the flowers. After a moment, she said,

"I forgive you, Nick. But that doesn't mean that we're gonna pick right up where we left off."

Nick shoved his hands into the pockets of his jacket to stop himself from wrapping his arms around Dallas. She looked so good to him.

"We've got enough to build on, Dallas," he said quietly. "People make mistakes. I made a mistake."

Something in Dallas's pretty light brown eyes softened.

"You can be a real jerk," she said. The words were harsh, but the tone wasn't.

"You're right," Nick agreed. "I can be."

"You're gonna have to work on that."

"I've already started."

The invisible wall that Dallas erected between them seemed to be crumbling.

"I've missed you so much, baby." Nick moved close enough to her that they were an arm's length away from each other. "I'm going to kiss you, Dallas."

She could have stopped him if she had really wanted to—but she didn't. Nick grabbed the front of her coat, pulled her into his universe, wrapped her up in his arms and kissed her like he had spent every second of every day missing her.

"Goddamn, Dallas." Nick held her tightly. "We've got to work this out."

She had taken her hat off so she could rest her head against Nick's chest. This was the most comfortable she had been in months. Without using words, Dallas nodded. Perhaps there would be more difficult times in their reunion, but this wasn't one of them. It was hard to remember why she was ever nervous about seeing Nick again. Being folded into his arms—having him kiss her and kissing him in return—felt as natural as breathing.

"What are you thinking?" Nick pressed her.

Dallas pulled back enough to be able to look at his face. "I was thinkin' that I'd love to have an indoor riding arena to train in right now."

It took a split second for Nick to follow her meaning; when it hit him, he kissed her hard, grabbed her hand and started to lead her out of the barn.

"Where're you takin' me?" She put her hat back on her head with a laugh.

"I want to show you something."

At the entrance of the barn, Nick moved behind her so he could guide her by her shoulders. "You have to close your eyes."

"Another surprise?"

"Of course."

"I thought we'd decided against those."

"No," Nick disagreed. "Close your eyes."

When she hesitated, he added, "This is a trust exercise. Do you trust me?"

"Is that a trick question?"

"Dallas! I'm trying to give you a present! Cooperate, please."

"Fine. My eyes are closed."

Nick led her out of the barn, the sound of ice-covered grass crunching beneath their feet.

"Okay," Nick said. "We're going to stop right here. Don't open your eyes until I tell you."

"Hurry up! I'm freezin' my butt off!"

"Hold your horses, woman."

She could hear Nick walking around her, and if she had read it correctly, he had stopped right in front of her.

"Okay," he said. "Open your eyes."

For the second time in a short span of time, Nick was back to kneeling on the ground in front of the woman he loved. This time, there was a box in his hand.

"Dallas." Nick opened the box. "I would consider it to be a great honor if you would consider becoming my wife."

Inside the box wasn't an engagement ring—instead, there was a key.

"Am I supposed to wear that?"

"You've got to say yes to find out," Nick laughed. "Okay—my knee is freezing. I have to stand up."

Dallas stared at the key in the box, thinking. She had told him along the way that she didn't want an engagement ring. What was the point of owning a ring that she would never wear—in her line of work, a ring on the finger could be dangerous. He had listened to her, which wasn't a surprise. But it hadn't occurred to her that he would propose on this trip—and it certainly didn't occur to her that he would propose within the first fifteen minutes of their reunion.

"Look." Nick must have been able to see her grappling with his proposal. "I know we have a lot to work out, but that's part of the fun, isn't it? I love you. And you love me. You *do* still love me, right?"

She gave him a slight nod of her head.

"Then just say that you'll *think* about marrying me, and I'll show you what your engagement key opens."

Nick waved the open box in front of her with a twinkle of excitement in his eyes. "You know you want to see what this key opens."

"I'll consider it," Dallas finally said. After all, she had been *considering* marrying Nick for months.

"That's not a no!" Nick hugged her tightly, kissed her, before he whistled loudly and yelled, "Clint! Let's show Dallas what's behind curtain number three!"

"It's a new car!" Nick had his arm around her shoulder.

Clint pulled into sight from behind a row of horse and cattle trailers; he was towing a flatbed trailer behind his truck. He waved at her from the driver's window.

"Well—a new truck, actually. A new old truck."

"That's for me?"

On the bed of the trailer was a refurbished antique truck, painted her favorite shade of turquoise blue. Nick had gotten her an engagement truck.

"Do you love it?"

Dallas nodded. It reminded her of her father. He had wanted to restore his antique trucks, and watching Davy's trucks being hauled away was one of the hardest parts of the cleanup at Lightning Rock.

Nick took her hand in his and led her over to the trailer. Clint got out of his truck.

"Thanks for your help, buddy." Nick shook Clint's hand.

"Glad to do it," Clint said to Nick. To her, Clint said, "Give the man a chance to make things up to you, Dallas."

She hugged her best friend before Clint went to join his wife and daughter in the main house.

Dallas climbed up onto the trailer to get a closer look at the truck. "Where did you find this?"

The restoration of the truck was impeccable. She'd only seen trucks rehabbed like this in Las Vegas. The truck looked like it had just been driven straight off a showroom floor in the 1950s.

"Lightning Rock," Nick said, watching her from the ground.

Dallas stopped moving, her hands resting on the hood of the truck. It took a lot to make her tear up; with tears in her eyes, she ran her hand over the hood of Davy's most prized possession. She had thought that it was lost to her forever.

Dallas hopped down off the trailer, threw herself into Nick's arms and gave him the first genuine hug since their fight in Chicago.

"I love you, Nick." Dallas rested her head against his chest. "Thank you."

Nick wiped her tears off her cheeks, held her face in his hands and looked down at her with love in his eyes. "I love you, Dallas. I'm not perfect…"

"Neither am I!"

"But I do love you."

Thanksgiving Day was a bustling, loud, chaotic affair at Bent Tree's main house. Nick's aunt Barbara was happier than he had seen her since he reunited with this side of his family. She was a woman who thrived when surrounded by her children and her grandchildren. The kitchen was filled with incredible smells of turkey basting, sage-bread stuffing cooking, apple, pumpkin and cherry pies cooling on racks. Pots of Brussels sprouts and mashed potatoes were being kept warm on the stove top; the sound of children playing, crying and laughing and multiple adult conversations overlapping blended together into one loud cacophonous din that *felt* the way a holiday should feel. At his parents' Lincoln Park mansion, Thanksgiving had always been a formal, quiet, well-ordered affair and the food was prepared by the cooks on duty. In Nick's opinion, a Bent Tree Thanksgiving beat his Lincoln Park Thanksgivings by a mile.

"What has Dallas done to you, Nicholas?" His older sister, Taylor, broke into his internal dialogue.

"What are you driving at?" Nick asked her.

"Well—you've been holding your niece for ten minutes now and you haven't broken out into hives or the sweats."

Nick laughed. "Don't read too much into it. Penny didn't have to eat, cry or be changed."

Taylor took her daughter into her arms and kissed her on her peaches-and-cream chubby cheek. Penny squealed and buried her head into her mom's blouse.

"Happy Thanksgiving, Nick." Taylor kissed him on the cheek.

"Happy Thanksgiving."

Luke and his wife, Sophia, arrived, followed by their three children.

"Oh! Sophia! I could sure use your hands right now to make the one-cup salad!"

Sophia, a pretty blonde with hazel-green eyes and a sweet disposition, gave him a quick hug in greeting and then went straight to her mother-in-law to help with the meal prep.

"Can I go outside with J.T. and Grandpa?" Luke's towheaded son, Danny, asked his father.

Luke gave his son the green light and the young boy ran out of the kitchen into the foyer.

"Don't forget your coat, Danny!" Sophia called after her son.

"Got it, Mom!" Danny called back, and then slammed the front door behind him.

Luke stood beside him, as inept with anything kitchen related as he was.

"It's good to see you and Sophia back together," Nick said to his cousin, quiet enough not to be heard with all the other noise in the room.

"I'm damn lucky she took me back," Luke said seriously, his thick, muscular arms crossed over his chest.

"How are you doing?"

Luke had shared with him on his last visit to the ranch that his PTSD had made married life nearly impossible.

"One day at a time, brother," Luke said. "I was accepted by K-9 Care—after the holidays, I'm going to be matched with a service dog."

"Congratulations, man. That's great news."

They caught up for a few minutes longer and then Luke headed outside to join his son, his father and his brother Tyler's stepson, who had pulled his snowmobile out of the shed. The one person Nick had been waiting to arrive showed up soon after—his younger sister, Casey, and her fiancé, Brock.

"Nick!" Casey hugged him tightly and enthusiastically as she always did.

Casey had a face full of freckles, wide emerald eyes

and a beautiful head of thick auburn hair. The family had been worried about Casey—she was a uterine cancer survivor and was still emotionally recovering from surgery. Taylor had let him know that Casey had been struggling with depression. But today, her eyes were bright and happy.

"You doing okay, munchkin?" he asked his slim-framed sister.

"I'm having a great day."

"Is Hannah coming today, Brock?" Barbara's voice cut through the other voices.

"She's with her mother in California." The ranch foreman snuck a biscuit out of a basket on the table.

"Oh—I was looking forward to seeing her," Barbara said. "But maybe it's just as well. It's loud here today."

Brock's daughter, Hannah, was on the autism spectrum and had difficulty with crowds and noise.

"Be sure to tell her happy Thanksgiving for me!" Nick's aunt added.

Nick had just finished hugging his younger sister when Dallas stepped into his arms. "Are you okay?"

"It's a lot different than Davy and me and two microwave turkey dinners."

Nick laughed as he hugged her tightly to him. "I'm not used to quite this many Brands at one time, but I have to say, I like it. Makes me think that I'd like to have a big family of my own one day."

"Hank. Hank?" Barbara looked around the kitchen for her husband. "Tyler, please go find your father! Where did he go? He knew we were about to eat!"

Tyler, known to be the easygoing son, reached

around his mother to pluck a Brussels sprout out of the pot and popped it into his mouth.

"You should have another glass of wine," Tyler said between chews. "It'll help you remember that holidays are supposed to be fun."

Barbara spun her tall son around and gave him a playful push. "Go!"

It wasn't easy to get all the Brands wrangled in the kitchen, but it finally happened. Barbara delegated jobs to each person, directing family members to wash their hands, take dishes to the table, and make sure everyone had a glass for wine, or water, or homemade root beer.

The last event was Hank taking the golden thirty-pound turkey out of the oven.

Nick stood behind his designated seat next to Dallas, and he, along with the rest of the family, clapped and whooped as Hank put the turkey on the table. He was about to make a preemptive reach for the one-cup salad when Barbara raised her voice to get everyone's attention.

His aunt's eyes were watery with emotion as she stood next to her husband at the head of the table and looked at her family. She put her hands together and rested her chin on her fingertips, appearing to get her emotions settled.

"It means so much to have you all here today." Her eyes drifted briefly to the empty seat that they had all agreed to leave empty for Daniel. "I want us to resurrect a Brand family tradition. Before we sit down to eat, I would like for all of us to share what we are most thankful for this year."

"I'll start," his aunt continued with an emotional

catch in her voice. "I'm thankful to have all of you here at Bent Tree Ranch for Thanksgiving. I am thankful for our ability to forgive each other, our ability to love one another. May we all see even more Brand family members around our Thanksgiving table next year."

One by one, all the Brands shared what they were thankful for the most.

"I'm thankful that we have set a date for our wedding." Josephine Brand, an attorney from San Diego, hugged her police officer fiancé. "By this time next year, I will be Mrs. Logan Brand-Wolf."

Jordan Brand, her arm linked with her husband Ian's arm followed her twin by saying, "I'm thankful that Ian has found his way back to photography, which is his life's passion. And I am super thankful that our application has been accepted by an adoption agency and we hope to adopt a sibling group next year!"

Tyler Brand was thankful to have been able to move his young family back to the ranch he loved; his heart had always been with Bent Tree Ranch, and with his being the next in line to inherit the ranch, his time living in Virginia had seemed like much too long for all of them.

Luke was thankful to have moved back with his wife and kids in their house outside Helena, just as he was thankful for having survived Afghanistan and Iraq, when so many of his friends and his own twin brother had not. He wasn't surprised when his sister Taylor was thankful that her husband, Clint, had decided to give up bull riding, or that she was thankful for their daughter, Penny. It had been her dream to be a mother and she considered Penny to be her miracle baby; in many ways, she was a miracle, having been born premature.

"I'm thankful for Hannah—for Brock—for surviving cancer—and…" Casey beamed at everyone at the table. "I'm thankful that we have begun the process of looking for a surrogate to carry our child."

Dallas was thankful for how the Brand family had cared for her father, thankful for the kindness he had shown her at Lightning Rock and thankful for how the entire family had taken her under their wings. And then it was his turn. His statement stood between a table full of hungry Brands and the delicious-smelling food on the table.

Nick threaded his fingers with Dallas's fingers. "I'm thankful for many things this year, but what I am most thankful for is the love of this incredible woman right here."

He looked into his cowgirl's eyes, finding it surprisingly easy to put his family in the background as he said, "I love you, Dallas. I hope I will be able to call you my wife one day."

"Happy Thanksgiving!" the entire family cheered after Hank led the family through a prayer.

Chair legs scraped across the floor, bowls were passed, silverware clinked against plates and children cried in their high chairs. As Nick scooped large helpings of one-cup salad onto his plate, he thought that this was exactly how he always wanted Thanksgiving to be—surrounded by his family, with the woman he loved by his side.

Dallas touched his leg with her hand to get his attention.

"What can I get for you?" he asked, thinking that she wanted a dish passed her way.

Dallas leaned in toward him, her eyes looking directly into his.

"Yes." She said one word.

"Yes?" He wanted to confirm that she was, quietly, in her own way, agreeing to be his wife.

"Yes," Dallas repeated, and then added in a whisper, "More than anything this year, Nick, I am thankful for you."

* * * * *

*If you loved Nick's story, don't miss out
on his sisters' stories in*
THE BRANDS OF MONTANA *miniseries:*
*MEET ME AT THE CHAPEL
HIGH COUNTRY BABY*

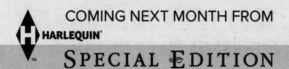

COMING NEXT MONTH FROM

HARLEQUIN®

SPECIAL EDITION

Available November 22, 2016

#2515 THE HOLIDAY GIFT
The Cowboys of Cold Creek • by RaeAnne Thayne
Neighboring rancher Chase Brannon has been a rock for Faith Dustin since her husband died, leaving her with two young children. Now Chase wants more. But Faith must risk losing the friendship she treasures and her hard-fought stability—and her heart—by opening herself to love.

#2516 A BRAVO FOR CHRISTMAS
The Bravos of Justice Creek • by Christine Rimmer
Ava Malloy is a widow and single mother who is not going to risk another heartbreak, but a holiday fling with hunky CEO Darius Bravo sounds just lovely! Darius wants to give her a Bravo under her tree—every Christmas. Can he convince Ava to take a chance on a real relationship or are they doomed to be a temporary tradition?

#2517 THE MORE MAVERICKS, THE MERRIER!
Montana Mavericks: The Baby Bonanza • by Brenda Harlen
Widowed rancher Jamie Stockton would be happy to skip Christmas this year, but Fallon O'Reilly is determined to make the holidays special for his adorable triplets—and for the sexy single dad, too!

#2518 A COWBOY'S WISH UPON A STAR
Texas Rescue • by Caro Carson
A Hollywood star is the last thing Travis Palmer expects to find on his ranch, so when Sophia Jackson shows up for "peace and quiet," he knows she must be hiding from something—or maybe just herself. There's definitely room on the ranch for Sophia, but Travis must convince her to make room in her heart for him.

#2519 THE COWBOY'S CHRISTMAS LULLABY
Men of the West • by Stella Bagwell
Widowed cowboy Denver Yates has long ago sworn off the idea of having a wife or children. He doesn't want to chance that sort of loss a second time. However, when he meets Marcella Grayson, he can't help but be attracted to the redheaded nurse and charmed by her two sons. When Marcella ends up pregnant, will Denver see a trap or a precious Christmas gift?

#2520 CHRISTMAS ON CRIMSON MOUNTAIN
Crimson, Colorado • by Michelle Major
When April Sanders becomes guardian of two young girls, she has no choice but to bring them up Crimson Mountain while she manages her friends' resort cabins. Waiting for her at the top is Connor Pierce, a famous author escaping his own tragedy and trying to finish his book. Neither planned on loving again, but will these two broken souls mend their hearts to claim the love they both secretly crave?

YOU CAN FIND MORE INFORMATION ON UPCOMING HARLEQUIN® TITLES, FREE EXCERPTS AND MORE AT WWW.HARLEQUIN.COM.

HSECNM1116

*Chase Brannon missed his first shot at a future with
Faith Dustin, but will the magic of the holiday season
give him a second chance?*

Read on for a sneak preview of
THE HOLIDAY GIFT,
the next book in New York Times *bestselling author
RaeAnne Thayne's beloved miniseries,*
THE COWBOYS OF COLD CREEK.

"You're the one who insisted this was a date-date. You
made a big deal that it wasn't just two friends carpooling
to the stock growers' party together, remember?"

"That doesn't mean I'm ready to start dating again, at
least not in general terms. It only means I'm ready to start
dating you."

There it was.

Out in the open.

The reality she had been trying so desperately to
avoid. He wanted more from her than friendship and she
was scared out of her ever-loving mind at the possibility.

The air in the vehicle suddenly seemed charged,
crackling with tension. She had to say something but had
no idea what.

"I… Chase—"

"Don't. Don't say it."

His voice was low, intense, with an edge to it she
rarely heard. She had so hoped they could return to the
easy friendship they had always known. Was that gone
forever, replaced by this jagged uneasiness?

"Say…what?"

"Whatever the hell you were gearing up for in that tone of voice like you were knocking on the door to tell me you just ran over my favorite dog."

"What do you want me to say?" she whispered.

"I sure as hell don't want you trying to set me up with another woman when you're the only one I want."

She stared at him, the heat in his voice rippling down her spine. She swallowed hard, not knowing what to say as awareness seemed to spread out to her fingertips, her shoulder blades, the muscles of her thighs.

He was so gorgeous and she couldn't help wondering what it would be like to taste that mouth that was only a few feet away.

She swallowed hard, not knowing what to say. He gazed down at her for a long, charged moment, then with a muffled curse, he leaned forward on the bench seat and lowered his mouth to hers.

Given the heat of his voice and the hunger she thought she glimpsed in his eyes, she might have expected the kiss to be intense, fierce.

She might have been able to resist that.

Instead, it was much, much worse.

It was soft and unbearably sweet, with a tenderness that completely overwhelmed her. His mouth tasted of caramel and apples and the wine he'd had at dinner—delectable and enticing—and she was astonished by the urge she had to throw her arms around him and never let go.

Don't miss
THE HOLIDAY GIFT by RaeAnne Thayne,
available December 2016 wherever
Harlequin® Special Edition books and ebooks are sold.

www.Harlequin.com

HSEEXP1116

THE WORLD IS BETTER WITH

Romance

Harlequin has everything from contemporary, passionate and heartwarming to suspenseful and inspirational stories.

Whatever your mood, we have romance when you need it, wherever you are!

HARLEQUIN®

A *Romance* FOR EVERY MOOD™

www.Harlequin.com

#RomanceWhenYouNeedIt

HARLEQUIN®

A *Romance* FOR EVERY MOOD™

JUST CAN'T GET ENOUGH?

Join our social communities
and talk to us online.

You will have access to the latest
news on upcoming titles and special
promotions, but most importantly,
you can talk to other fans about your
favorite Harlequin reads.

Harlequin.com/Community

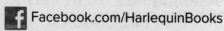

Facebook.com/HarlequinBooks

Twitter.com/HarlequinBooks

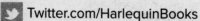

Pinterest.com/HarlequinBooks

READERSERVICE.COM

Manage your account online!

- Review your order history
- Manage your payments
- Update your address

> *We've designed the*
> *Reader Service website*
> *just for you.*

Enjoy all the features!

- Discover new series available to you, and read excerpts from any series.
- Respond to mailings and special monthly offers.
- Connect with favorite authors at the blog.
- Browse the Bonus Bucks catalog and online-only exculsives.
- Share your feedback.

Visit us at:
ReaderService.com